Disquiet

Disquiet

stories from a law library

Dan Hibshman

Secret Goldfish Press

ISBN: 9798613960743

Cover and courthouse photos by Tom Liden
Author photo by Leslie Kirkpatrick

Secret Goldfish Press
1001 Recreation Rd.
Ukiah, CA 95482
bookem@pacific.net

To Leslie

devoted, loving, supportive
strong, independent
always

Contents**

** Between the stories are sketches of more
visitors to the library.

Introduction

The County

Everything in the West was big; Manzanita County was a huge land area, larger than the entirety of such East Coast states as Delaware or Rhode Island. It was one of the original counties that banded together to form the state of California in 1850, and at the time a few lawmakers lobbied for naming Grant City as the state capital. Since those days Sacramento had become a metropolis, while Grant City had grown modestly and remained a quiet county seat.

The indigenous population, as all across the West and indeed all the United States, had been treated harshly from the time of white settlers' arrival. There were still Native Americans in the county, proud of their heritage, yet the assimilation enforced by the newcomers had wreaked havoc on nearly all their lives.

The topography was rugged. Pioneer families, now into fourth and fifth generations on the land, had built their identities out of hard work and endurance surviving on it. There were very steep mountains, not as high as the Sierra Nevada but snow-covered along their ridgelines in winter and into spring; thick forests of conifer trees dotted with sawmills (the methods for falling old-growth timber in the days before chainsaws

were epic); rivers descending from the mountains and—
at least in those earlier days—teeming with fish; a few
widely spaced valleys of moderate size, suitable for
cattle and sheep ranching and for fruit agriculture: apple
then pear orchards, most recently vineyards.

On its southwest the county bordered by far the
largest natural lake in the state. Along its shoreline a
string of settlements developed from the late 1800s on,
first with fishing camps, later with summer resorts, in
recent decades with year-round artist colonies. The
natural beauty of the setting—combined with
skyrocketing rents in California's big cities—created a
cultural oasis. Elsewhere, in the county's vast interior,
idealists from the generation of the 1960s and '70s
experimented continuously with ways of making
Manzanita home.

The history of transportation in the county helped
explain why its population remained small: there were
no easy ways to move what was produced there to the
far more populous world beyond. After the horse-and-
stagecoach era, roads for cars and trucks had gradually
improved, from muddy ruts impassable in winter to a
few snaking paved highways. But even with these,
distance and time undercut profit. Attempts at building
and maintaining rail lines were also repeatedly
undertaken, only sooner or later to succumb to
rockslides and tunnel cave-ins.

Year after year go-getters in the county (using public
funds) renewed efforts to build the local economy,

particularly to attract tourists. And people did come, for Manzanita County was a very beautiful place. But so too were numerous other parts of California, and the hoped-for boost never really materialized. Life went on, people muddling through, not so different from everywhere else.

The Courthouse

The Manzanita County Courthouse was an ungainly amalgamation of two buildings, one from approximately the turn of the twentieth century, the other a bigger, taller addition from the '50s. The former faced west onto Pine Street in downtown Grant City: a distinguished-looking edifice, classical in architecture, dark sandstone in material. Adjacent to the entrance and incised in stone were the last names, preceded by two initials, of the county supervisors who approved its construction in 1904.

Because the later addition rose above and partially enclosed it, the original structure was somewhat difficult to see just for itself. Clearly, it was a quite small building which for decades had served as the entire seat of county government, not only courts but all county departments. By the '50s, operations inside it must have outgrown available space, and so the relatively large addition, facing east onto Main Street, was erected. Viewed from the north it had the shape (from the south the reverse) of a capital L, its base at street level, then its riser climbing well above the older structure's classical roof. It must be true that its architects thought well of it, but by early in the twenty-first century this opinion was hard to recapture. Yes, perhaps there was something mid-century "modern" about it, but modernity seemed to be a surplus of plainness, achieved in dull white concrete, greenish panels, and around the entrance a lot of glass.

Although the two portions of the courthouse were built at the same elevation, on the same level ground, their interiors didn't mesh at all, which handed down a legacy of confusion about the numbering of floors. The culprit in this was a likable feature of the addition; the east entrance was at the top of two flights of outdoor stairs. This in turn created a public space: the courthouse steps, that traditional setting where "the people" could exercise their rights of assembly, protest, and speech. (Far more mundanely, the steps were the site of certain public business transactions, such as auctions of defaulted property.)

In any event, by setting the courthouse entrance so high on that east side, the architects determined that a person entering there was about a floor-and-a-half above the old Pine Street entrance on the west. Furthermore, the staircases inside the addition were a mix of long ones and short ones, partly to accomplish meshing the two buildings, partly to create a tall, resonant stairwell inside the addition's open interior.

The resulting amalgam was numbered "basement" to "fifth floor," but some were just half-floors, leaving people unfamiliar with the building continually confused. To Henry Daniels, the law librarian, on some slow days it seemed the totality of his work consisted of giving directions.

Much longer ago, during the second half of the nineteenth century, an entirely different courthouse stood in downtown Grant City. It was a frilly Victorian, the "footprint" of which, as opposed to being where its classical successor still stood, was on the mathematical center of the entire block surrounded by Pine, Perkins, Main, and Oak.

In the late 1980s the County of Manzanita built an administrative center on the outskirts of Grant City and moved nearly all its departments there. This left the courthouse to the courts, plus a few county offices, primarily the District Attorney, whose existence had everything to do with the courts.

Also around then a vast consolidation took place throughout California. What had formerly been a network of "justice courts," held in numerous small communities around Manzanita and every other county, was eliminated. The local courts became an arm of state government called "Superior Court of California, County of Manzanita." In turn this changed the employment status of the bureaucracy: all the clerks, court reporters, bailiffs, and translators became employees of the state, not the county.

Another cadre of courthouse regulars were the security guards, posted immediately after September 11, 2001. They were employed by neither the state nor the county but by a private corporation. Beefing up security amounted to further modification of the building itself. The entrance from the north, on Perkins Street, was permanently closed. People could come in through the east and south entrances but metal detectors were installed at both; except for very familiar faces that the guards waved through, people's pockets had to be emptied and their belts, sometimes boots, removed.

Use of the entrance from the west, the classical doorway on Pine Street, was drastically limited. Now it was exclusively for the use of sheriff's deputies transporting inmates from (and back to) county jail, the latter arriving for some court appearance. This created one of the most memorable courthouse scenes: lines of inmates in orange or red jail garb, shoes with no laces, wrists and ankles shackled, shuffling slowly into the basement. Some of them, a few at a time, boarded an elevator that would take them to a courtroom on the third or fifth floor; others, whose appearances weren't scheduled till later in the day, were herded into a "holding pen," also in the basement. The first time Henry Daniels came along at just such a moment of inmates' arrival, the deputy barked at him, "Sir! Please wait!"

Outside and nearby, across Oak Street from the southern entrance, was a commercial establishment that, in light of all the business it did with denizens of the courthouse, might as well have been part of the judicial system. Schindler's Bakery and Cafe was the place to go on a coffee break, maybe for a sandwich, or to buy a loaf of bread. Vehicle traffic on Oak Street was far busier during the day than before or after work hours. Even so, courthouse people barely waited before crossing it directly to Schindler's double doors.

The Law Librarian

Despite his job title, Henry Daniels didn't consider himself a librarian. With past stints of varying length as clerk at a natural-foods store, journalist, encyclopedia salesman, book editor, community gardener, and writer of publicity, he had mainly been a teacher.

Teaching began after college at an inner-city high school in the Midwest. Then, turns of event in those long-ago days resulted in an abrupt move to California, where he landed a job as the fifth-grade teacher in Apple Valley, Manzanita County—"the" because every grade at that school had only one class. In a crowded room overlooking a cow pasture he taught all subjects (except art and music) to 27 ten- and eleven-year-olds, even coached after-school sports. His own young age made him feel more like their older brother than the adult in charge of their classroom.

At the time of the move to California Daniels was married, to another teacher. In this place so different from anything they'd known, life was very new and stimulating for both of them: they found a house in the country to rent, adopted a golden retriever, swam in sparkling rivers, planted a big garden, chainsawed and split firewood, raised two goats, harvested and canned pears, picked blackberries and made jam. During summers off they went camping on long road trips. Friends from "back East" came to visit and were wowed by the rural West; the couple glowed in what seemed their success.

After four years at Apple Valley Elementary, restless, recognizing he'd been in school continuously since his own little-boyhood, Daniels decided to quit. His wife at first was supportive, and her income continued. With an influx of available time, having always dreamed of fame as a writer, he set to work on what he hoped would become a novel. But all the hours he spent alone were changing him, he realized, and he could tell also that his wife, while still teaching, was heading in her own directions. Perhaps, he reflected decades later, their lives had been *too* new.

The marriage foundered, then ended. He moved away from what for him became severe claustrophobia in Apple Valley, first to Johnsville, next to Comstock, then to Grant City. His far-from-finished novel in a box, he went back to work for many years in that miscellany of jobs, often employed in two at once.

In those days, attempting to cover the entire county there existed an "alternative" weekly called *The Manzanita Bark*, whose offices occupied the second floor of an old, yellow-painted-brick building on Grant City's Main Street. (The building was owned, and the first floor used, by the International Order of Odd Fellows.) This was just a few steps from the Manzanita County Courthouse, which at that time, besides the courts, housed most of the county departments. Newly drawn into the small world of local journalism, cub reporter Henry Daniels' first "beat" was the Board of Supervisors, which met in a room that years later was converted into Courtroom C. He watched, listened, and took notes on the proceedings of the BoS, which he converted into a weekly column titled "Supes Notes." Also he copy-edited, proofread, wrote other news, feature stories, play reviews, once even covered a murder trial. In later years—the *Bark* folded after only five or six in operation—he recalled his work on it as the best job he ever had. Paid to write! Scenes and people inside and around the courthouse became exceptionally familiar, and at the *Bark* he was part of a group that felt like family: photographers, editors, other writers, people in layout, paste-up, ad sales.

After the paper's pathetic demise, he returned to teaching. This was English at Manzanita Community College, where he was defined as "adjunct" faculty: a part-timer limited to at most three courses per semester; poorly paid (for classroom time only, nothing for all the prep); without any health, retirement, or other benefit. In parts of California, adjunct faculty were known as "freeway flyers" for their hustling to teach at several colleges and make more money. Manzanita CC was so far away from other two-year schools—nor were there freeways—that Daniels chose not to go that route.

After seventeen years as a part-timer (plus his nearly always working a second job), a full-time position opened in the English department—the chance he'd been waiting for. Extremely confident he was the best candidate, he applied and after a long wait was interviewed. Someone else was hired. Afterwards, he was shocked to receive a curt note from the department head stating that there would no longer be *any* English classes for him at Manzanita Community College.

Later, someone offhandedly suggested that becoming a paralegal could offer him a new direction. He completed the required course work online at home, even as he continued substituting at Grant City High School; before long a Certificate of Completion in Paralegal Studies joined his dusty collection of advanced degrees.

Residence in Manzanita County nearly guaranteed he wouldn't find full-time work there as a paralegal. But just as he hadn't been a freeway flyer, Daniels was unwilling to commute to a big city where there would be far more legal business. Even so, he attempted to market himself and did land some freelance work, enough to keep him going. Each job was different, as was each attorney, and each experience helped make concrete the very abstract education he'd gotten online. Serendipity drew him to the Manzanita County Law Library, located in Room 219 of the courthouse. Eight months later, above all to exchange the uncertainty of freelancing for the assurance of regularly scheduled (part-time, of course) employment, he became an assistant to Edward Donovan, the law librarian at the time.

Teaching, now at a small private school, continued to be his other job. He brought student essays and tests with him to the library and, during lulls in library business, marked and graded them. He furthered his recent education by close reading of legal newspapers and magazines and by building his skill at legal research.   In part this meant he studied statutes and case decisions, on the Internet or in the hardbound volumes on the library's shelves.   It was strenuous mental exercise to fo follow the logic of legal reasoning and the syntax of legal writing; he enjoyed the workout.

Threshold

THE LAW LIBRARY had one door, which served as both entrance and exit. There was a second door, which led to the sanctum of a judge's chambers, but for many years it had been locked, in fact also barricaded by a cart of used law books for sale at five dollars apiece. Naturally, the one door was where the law librarian opened the library five mornings a week, and where one of his assistants closed it at the end of each day. But most significantly it was the threshold crossed by patrons of the place.

A few of these were regulars, particularly local attorneys who came to do legal research, use the copy machine, perhaps review notes (on their yellow 8½ x14 legal pads) before appearing in court. There were also non-attorney regulars, people so absorbed with their own cases that they very frequently took advantage of the library's resources; they searched for material to reinforce arguments that would, they believed, triumph in front of a judge.

These two types of regulars were of some interest to him, but because they rarely needed the librarian to do anything other than receive payment for copies, they tended to fade into the very quiet background of the place. Yes, because it *was* a library, quiet was appropriate. But without enough to engage him, and with very little managerial business to attend to, Henry Daniels came to feel that his job lacked meaning.

Thus the unfamiliar presence of non-regulars crossing the threshold came to take on special importance. Each

1

one of these men and women represented an opportunity for him to be of service, much more so than they themselves probably realized. At a minimum he tried to be a good listener; operating inside of but apart from bureaucracies that tended to be short if not impatient, he struck many as a sympathetic ear. If it was possible and likely to be useful, he guided the person to some reference book in the library that would provide, if not a solution, then at least some education. Or he'd offer encouragement by suggesting a different office or agency to visit, somewhere in the courthouse or very nearby, whose mission was to assist in cases like the one at hand.

The library was L-shaped, its two legs of about equal length. The wall furthest from the entrance was glazed with tall windows that looked to the outside of the courthouse, through the sparse, evergreen branches of an old Pacific silver fir, down to the corner of Oak and Pine streets. On their breaks, several female clerks from inside the building took drags of their cigarettes there, as did a woman criminal-defense lawyer whose office was across Pine. Parking spaces nearby were reserved for law enforcement: sheriff's deputies, Highway Patrol officers, police from Grant City or Johnsville or Comstock, typically summoned by the prosecution to appear in court. Windows on two other walls of the library, the inner sides of the two legs of the L, both looked out upon a large unit of the building's heating/cooling system. Occasionally, maintenance workers would reach it by descending a metal staircase from above. An ominous—but also seemingly unnecessary—fake raptor perched beside that staircase.

Two desks near the threshold were reserved for use by Daniels or whichever employee was working at any given time. On one sat a computer containing files of the library's business, which the librarian needed to access occasionally. The other, closer to the door, was where he sat when he had nothing else to do, but which also put himself in position to encounter anyone entering.

Sometimes the most interesting activity in the vicinity of the library was happening just outside it. The double doors of Courtroom E were a few feet away across a narrow hall, and as participants and spectators in a matter about to be heard in that court arrived, the overall volume of their conversation steadily increased, amplified by the tall stairwell of the amalgamated courthouse. It was easy for the librarian to identify attorneys in the swelling crowd, for they were always the best dressed; in addition, they spoke with a level of comfort and confidence characteristic of their profession. In Henry Daniels' eyes the stereotype of lawyer as shark seemed overly broad, but from his desk he did routinely see evidence that had given rise to it.

Sometimes as they waited to enter Courtroom E, or on a break from proceedings there, ordinary citizens would approach the threshold but stop short of entering, almost as if a force field blocked them.

"Am I allowed to come in here?" one might ask.

"Sure," Daniels would answer. "Open to the public. Come on in."

Then, advancing uneasily into the room and glancing up and around at the tall shelves, the person might say, "Have you read all these books?"

"Yep," he'd reply, trying with his inflection to let the person know he was joking.

This feint sometimes was but sometimes wasn't successful. In either case, the visit quickly ended when the person, either lacking further interest or summoned by re-opening of the courtroom, turned and walked out.

One day a woman entered. There was an air of both tension and exhaustion about her. Her thick graying hair, pulled back tightly and bound by a brass clip, hung half-way down her back on top of a puffy black sleeveless vest. Under the vest was a blue turtleneck. She was carrying a few rumpled papers in hands that emerged from the turtleneck's long sleeves. The skin of her hands was rough and weathered, as was her face, whose features retained the handsome lines of a distant youth.

She stood uneasily in front of the desk and looked at Henry Daniels, but her glance quickly roamed the room and back into the hall before returning to look at him again.

"I don't know if I've come to the right place," she said very softly, looking down as she shuffled the papers.

"Well," he said, "for now let's figure you haven't come to the wrong one." After a moment's hesitation during which neither of them spoke, he continued, "What's going on? Maybe if you tell me something about your situation, I can do something to help you deal with it."

"You make it sound so simple. If it were simple, I wouldn't be standing here." Her voice had risen and there was anger in it.

"I'm sorry," he said. "Whatever it is, I'm sure it's not simple . . . easy. I guess I didn't . . . do it very well, but I was trying to encourage you."

"Is there a women's room?" she asked abruptly.

"Down the hall, go past the stairs, it's on your right."

She disappeared. He was surprised to see the papers she'd been holding still on the desk. Aware of his innate,

4

potentially rude nosiness, he thought that whatever information they carried almost certainly pertained to what was going on with her, so from his chair he attempted to read the page on top. It appeared to have been torn from a spiral notebook, its left edge ragged where once it had been smooth; most of the surface was covered in large, somewhat careless handwriting in red ink. He didn't want to disturb the little stack, so he tried to read just that top one, from a distance and, because of the position in which she'd left the stack, upside down.

It appeared to be part of a letter or journal, but he couldn't see well enough to get beyond such a general impression. That raised a practical, ethical, even slightly comical dilemma: should he and could he—knowing she might return at any moment—get up and read rapidly from a better angle? If he went ahead he'd learn more. On the other hand, leaving the papers alone might redound to his credit, in some small way contributing when she returned to her confidence that she could trust him.

As a half-measure, as if there were a task he needed to perform there, he thought of going to the copy machine a few feet away, where the different angle would enable him, looking back toward the front desk, to read the paper right-side up. But before he could act, Wallace Vaughn, a non-attorney regular who had entered the library about forty-five minutes before the woman did, settled in at the copy machine.

From years of experience with him, the librarian knew Vaughn might occupy the machine for a long time. It was Vaughn's habit to do voluminous research on his way toward writing extraordinarily lengthy briefs, which rarely succeeded when Vaughn eventually submitted them.

5

Despite these repeated setbacks, he routinely bragged about the quality of his motions, always in part basing his confidence on their length. He never needed the librarian's help to find legal materials, and he was expert at using the copier. Far more distinctive than these habits, though, was something in his personality which, in the present instance of the distressed woman, the librarian didn't want to trigger. The man had a very debatable sense of himself as charming, and he tended to make conversation with anyone and everyone in his sphere. For this reason, wanting to prevent contact between the two of them, the librarian was preemptively trying to shield her, but Vaughn's position at the copy machine made this more difficult.

"Oh!" she exclaimed as she re-entered the room and spotted the papers. "I'm not usually like this. But for the past few days I haven't been myself."

Daniels considered making a joke about the papers' excellence but immediately saw the foolishness in that. So he was taken aback when she volunteered, "What did you think of my writing?"

"I . . . I *was* interested to know what's there," he stammered, "but I knew it was none of my business."

Something seemed to have changed in her since she'd left and come back—a greater playfulness perhaps?—which tended to relieve the severity of the first impression she made. But he didn't particularly trust these inklings; rather, there remained the welcome work of learning more. Many times in the past he'd invited someone standing where she stood to take the seat next to him, at the desk on which stood the library's reserved computer. Sitting there, he knew, changed the dynamics for the better; both people were seated then, and the library patron didn't feel as exposed as at first.

"Would you like to sit down?" he invited her, gesturing to the other swivel chair.

She looked around the library before wordlessly answering yes. The papers were again in one of her hands as she moved around the front desk. Turning partway in order to face her, he noticed that the thighs of her faded jeans were smudged with black lines, evidence, he thought, of woodstove heating. On her feet were a pair of scuffed workboots that rose above her ankles, veterans, probably, of years in the hills.

A change in her manner seemed evident when she spoke, the earlier self-absorbed tone eclipsed by her saying,

"You probably get tired of people coming in here and telling you their troubles."

"That's not at all how I look at it," Daniels replied. "I can't necessarily do anything to help, but I do like to try. And frankly, it makes the job more interesting than it is most of the time." He realized, but said nothing of it to her, that some of the people in those impromptu situations were mentally ill, and in fact that their illness could wear out their welcome. Even then, there were times he believed he'd offered at the least an opportunity to be heard.

"What do you think I need to know?" he continued. "Or maybe something in those papers would be useful to look at."

"I've lived in this county a long time," she slowly began. "For a few years I lived on the lake, with some other people. But then I decided I wanted to be inland, and

7

alone. I bought eighty acres above Apple Valley. You know where that is, don't you?"

"Once upon a time I used to live in Apple Valley."

"My place is at the end of a long dirt road. Years ago, I built a steel gate across the road, and when I'm not there the gate is locked." She shuffled the papers and waited before speaking some more. "I didn't move up there to be a dope grower. Yeah, I always had a few plants in with the vegetables, and a few more among the fruit trees in my orchard. But nothing like what's out there—everywhere!— now.

"There used to be a huge ranch at the north end of the valley, the ranchers raised sheep, over many generations. As far as I can tell, there wasn't any dope growing in the old days. Years must have gone by when their biggest problem was coyotes, I don't know, the occasional runaway dogs. But somehow, not long before I bought my place, their operation fell apart. Maybe the younger generation didn't want to ranch any more, I don't know. The people logged a few stands of timber to get the rest of what they could out of the land, then put the whole place up for sale." An expression on her face commented on that history, silently.

"No buyers! I think a few of the family went on living for a while in the big house on the valley floor, but the rest, and then I believe all of them, moved away. So nothing was happening on all those acres up above. Except. When this big-time dope scene got going, a bunch of people—I have my suspicions but I'm not sure who they are—figured out the land up there was . . . available." She sighed and then in a breaking voice cackled, "The rebirth of agriculture!"

8

She looked at the librarian to gauge how he was reacting. He pursed his lips, made a conscious effort not to look down or away: I'm listening, was the message he tried to send.

Just then someone else unfamiliar entered, a youngish man in a hurry: "Where's Courtroom G?"

The librarian told the woman, "I'll be right back," then stood and accompanied the man outside to a staircase. "Go up there, straight ahead, and you'll see signs for F and G." The man took the stairs three at a time, neither looking back nor saying more.

A small crowd was milling in the hall in front of Courtroom E. He had to slow down and weave among them in order to reach the library. Not far distant he heard the booming laugh of a lawyer, locally famous not only for that laugh.

In the library he was suddenly dismayed to see that the woman was no longer in the chair and, much more so, to find her in conversation with Wallace Vaughn. Even though Vaughn's lawbooks were still piled on the table beside the copy machine, and its lid was lifted (both suggesting he was in the middle of a copy job), he was talking with her at the rear of the library, beside the table where he habitually sat. Besides Daniels' earlier intuition about the likelihood of Vaughn's communicating with the woman, he realized he felt proprietary. When he'd been briefly interrupted and needed to leave the room, he'd been doing his proper job; *he* was the appropriate person to be connecting with her. So Vaughn's characteristic behavior irked him more than usual. Moreover, fully aware that the helping aspect of the job was what most appealed to him about it, at some deeper level and only partly conscious of it, he felt attracted to her.

Over time he'd learned how, when necessary, to wield the authority of his position. He turned to exercising it now. "Did you finish your copying, Wallace? If you're done, then let's get a count of how many copies you made, and you should take the books back. Or if you're not done, please finish. I think you know things can get confused if someone else comes in and wants to make copies while you're still at it."

The faint snapping of this whip brought Vaughn to the front again, but not before he first said something more to the woman, too soft for Daniels to hear. She remained in the area where she'd been standing, scanning the spines of the volumes nearest her on the shelves, seemingly without focus. The right thing to do, Daniels thought, was to leave her alone, at least for the time being. Yet this opposed his inclination to go to her and resume their conversation. He imagined moving to the chair where she'd been and logging on to the computer in front of it, to check on some library business. But sitting there might dissuade her from returning. Turning further away from her direction, he sat at the front desk again, opened its left middle drawer, and took out business that didn't urgently require his attention.

She remained in the same spot for what he thought, after repeated looks over his shoulder, was an inordinately long time. Was she lost in thought—spacing out?—or was she waiting for Vaughn? Daniels stood up, walked partway to the rear of the library, and asked, "Can I help you find something?"

With her head indicating Vaughn, who was still at the copy machine, she said, "He said *he* could."

10

Flustered but wanting to not show it, the librarian asked, "With what? How would he know what you need?"

"Do *you*?" she replied, in a tone he couldn't help hearing as a putdown.

Now there was tension between them there hadn't been before. He spoke as calmly as he could. "You know I was trying to learn about your situation. I don't see how anyone could help you without understanding that first."

"Of course," she said, more pleasantly than he expected. "But then you had to leave." Vaughn was still making copies.

"I told you I'd come right back. And I did."

"Yes, but when you left he came over. And it was like I'd been talking to him the whole time. He must have been eavesdropping or something." At this she even laughed.

Recognizing evidence of Vaughn's too-familiar manner, Daniels held in a groan. "Look," he told her, "I'm not a lawyer, and a basic principle of the job of law librarian is to not act as if you are one. Under any circumstances, the most I can do is listen to you and then try to steer you in a useful direction." Now he lowered his voice as he stepped closer to her. "But *he*'s not a lawyer either." For an instant he looked directly at her.

"You're a free agent in this," he continued. "You can go wherever you want with it. I just want you to know I'm very interested to hear more from you, if you want to tell me. And I *would* like to try to help."

With that he returned to the desk with the library-business computer, sat down, and logged on. Vaughn was still at the copy machine; it was impossible to know when he'd be finished. Briefly glancing beyond the computer monitor, the librarian saw that the woman had moved

11

further away, now in front of the tall windows that looked outside the courthouse. For a while these three figures remained in place.

The day's email presented the librarian with information and a few tasks to perform. As one member of a network of all the county law librarians in the state, he read messages addressed to every member of the network. Sometimes these were lightweight workplace greetings, such as "Happy Birthday" to so-and-so in a Central Valley county. Others were requests for help finding information: a very old court decision, or an article in a law review, something a patron somewhere was seeking. Daniels was curious about the content of the sought material, and he admired the cooperative spirit of the other librarians, but he also assumed the limited resources in "his" library would make the item impossible to find there. In fact, he'd gotten so used to people in the state's biggest law libraries answering the requests that he didn't try. Instead, he anticipated later reading someone's cheery "Thank You!" after the requested material was sent.

A few of the messages he recognized as bills. In order to pay them, he'd need to print out the invoice attached to the message. With a mixed sense of self-inflated importance and managerial failure to share knowledge with assistants, he realized he was the only person who knew the click-by-click procedures and passwords needed before pressing "print."

Once a month there was a message he'd come to dread: a statement of the amount of revenue the law library would be receiving from California's courts-administration bureau for that month. This figure represented close to 100% of the library's operating budget (accumulated income from book sales and use of the copy machine amounting to extremely little).   For months on end the dollar figure in the message was so low that he considered it unsustainable for much longer—or else the library's doors would remain open only on a sort of starvation diet. Nothing could be done to affect this crucial number, it being dictated entirely by outside forces. So the subject placed a great weight on his morale, compounding the boredom and sense of uselessness he too often felt sitting alone in the place.

"I guess you wanted to hear more," the woman said. He was startled to discover her standing right beside him. It wasn't uncommon for him to be so absorbed with studying the computer screen or paperwork that he didn't hear someone's approach. The difference in their relative positions changed her appearance slightly; she seemed taller. He was looking up at her now, without a desk between them, and he grew more conscious of her effect on him.

"That's true," he managed to say after the mild shock wore off. "Would you like to sit over here this time?" but then he realized he preferred she sit where he was: something would be off about her being at the front desk. "No," he corrected himself as he stood. "You sit here."

"I told you about my gate, didn't I?"

"Yes, but how does that connect with the land, the old sheep ranch?"

"The gate's not keeping them out. 'They'—the growers—just go around it. They have ATVs and just go around. Sometimes, when I'm there, I hear those machines. And it's easy to see the tire tracks and where grass gets pressed down."

13

"There's no fence?"

"What there was never amounted to much. It was stakes spaced pretty far apart, holding up one loose strand of barbed wire. Now a big section has been torn down. A couple of stakes are on the ground, broken, and the wire is cut."

"How much do you know about where they're going? I mean, is it way beyond your place? or pretty close? Do you know if they have other ways—from different directions—to get there"

"I don't. But I've gotta believe I'm their main way in and out. When I've been home, it's, like, a couple of times a day. But I haven't been sleeping at home every night lately. I have a friend in town."

"You said you have ideas—'suspicions'—about who they are." He wondered about the identity of the friend.

"Yes, I did say that. But I don't want to talk about it . . . them."

He didn't say anything. It made no sense to press her.

"What's on the papers?" he asked, attempting both to change the subject and keep their conversation going.

"Oh, I don't really think it amounts to much more than what I've already been telling you. I figured I'd need to explain the situation to somebody, sometime, so I wrote down what's happening."

"May I read it? Do you mind showing me?"

"I guess not," she answered. Handing the sheaf to him, she stood up, then drifted again toward the rear of the library.

His eyes scanned the page on top; he could quickly tell that what she'd said about the contents was true. By the middle of the next page, he thought he knew perhaps even more than was written down. He noted too the tendency of her loopy red ink to drift downward as the lines advanced from left to right, and the occasional spelling error: how, he couldn't help but wonder, could she spell it "Apple Vally"? He remembered her saying she hadn't been herself lately.

Simultaneously, he was thinking again of the positions of the three people in the library. Was Vaughn still at the copy machine? No—here he came. In his odd and cheerful way he announced, "I made 47 copies. I may make more later, but I know you like me to stay current, so I'll pay for these now." He put a twenty-dollar bill on the front desk. "And I'd like to pay all the outstanding IOUs of other people, and also make a donation."

Generous as Vaughn's offer seemingly was, the announcement meant at least two interruptions for Daniels, and, under the circumstances with the enigmatic woman, neither was welcome. First, it was the librarian's routine not to take the patron's word for how many copies he or she had made but rather to go to the machine and use its counter to determine the number for certain. He set the woman's papers down and went to the machine, which verified the accuracy of Vaughn's 47. Then he returned to the desk and reached for the binder in which the ongoing tally of various transactions (copies, computer printouts, book sales, donations) was recorded. He wrote down the machine's counter number, double-checking that it was 47 higher than the previous one on the page.

Second, as he reached for a paper-clipped collection of IOU slips, despite Vaughn's stated intent Daniels knew in advance this was going to be annoying. The reasons were complicated: because the librarian himself and his assistants were inconsistent keeping track of the debts;

15

because the amounts were as small as a dime and as large as several dollars; and because the people who'd written and signed the slips ranged from the penniless to the scoundrel to the affluent patron who discovered the library didn't accept credit cards. Daniels didn't want to scatter this collection onto the desk in order to arrive at a total amount owed, partly because of that complexity, but even more so because he didn't want Vaughn peering into the library's operation.

So he said to him, "I don't have the IOU number right now. And, you know, some of the people who write IOUs can easily pay—they just haven't done it yet. How much did you want to donate?"

"Why don't you just keep the twenty dollars," said Vaughn. "Like I said, I'm going to make more copies later, so part of this can be advance payment on that. And you can add up, or just estimate, the IOUs."

The conversation was, at least in Daniels' recollection, reenactment of similar exchanges the two of them had had before in the library. Like other components of Vaughn's behavior, the IOUs-payment plan defined him as quirky. This sort of thing was usually manageable, a regular fact of life and work in the place. But now, with the woman also there, the librarian perceived more than the usual forces were at work.

Where was she? He wasn't sure. Having concluded the conversation, Vaughn returned to the copy machine, scooped up an armload of books, and headed back to "his" table. The librarian needed to make a few decisions, at least preliminary ones, about dealing with Vaughn's intended transaction. To determine the time—to track the people, as well—he turned his head to view the clock on the wall above the used-book cart: 11:45.

Experience had taught him not to expect Valerie, the assistant who normally worked Tuesday and Thursday afternoons, to arrive before the stroke of noon, when she was supposed to begin her shift. Now he could see he'd need to summarize the situation with Vaughn's payment plan to her, and, because there were a couple other pieces of information he needed to convey to Valerie, he predicted he was unlikely to leave before about 12:15. But Valerie breezed across the threshold about ten minutes before noon.

"I was finished with an errand down the street," she explained (a quality in her voice often struck Daniels as insincere), "so I thought I'd come in early. Besides, I've got a lot of my own stuff to do, and I wanted to get started. It's going to take awhile."

His surprise at Valerie's early arrival probably wouldn't, under normal circumstances, have remained with him for long. As part of the typical mid-day transition, she had her habits of setting down a large handbag on a medium-sized filing cabinet and then making very small talk, both of which she proceeded to do. But today, with the Apple Valley woman in the library, he realized he felt very different about Valerie's being there. Though in fact she and Vaughn had some history of conflict with each other, at this moment he saw the two of them as quite similar: interrupters of his effort to hear more of the woman's story. Seated nearby at another computer (as would be ordinary behavior within their little workplace), Valerie would be sure to pay at least some attention to such out-of-the-ordinary conversation. Daniels recognized again his desire to shield it from others' ears.

He went back to the task at hand. He had roughly calculated when he glanced through them that the total debt in the current IOUs was more than $7.00; he was *not* going to do precise arithmetic with them right now but would leave such pesky nickel-and-diming until the next day. He decided to assign the value of $5.30 to the IOUs he would allow Vaughn to cover. His reasoning: $4.70 (for the 47 copies) + $5.30 = $10.00. That meant Vaughn would have ten more dollars out of his twenty to pay for some combination of more copies and a donation. Or, if the sum of the latter two came to more than $10, he could dig into his wallet again.

Daniels stood up and turned toward the rear of the library but was uncertain what to do next. The woman's papers were still lying where he'd left them. Should he walk them back to her? Even though he'd told her she was a "free agent," he knew he didn't want to see her talking to Vaughn. No matter what, he realized with an unexpected sense of relief, he needed to communicate with Valerie. So he sat down again at the front desk and on a small rectangle of scrap paper wrote the key numbers in his decision about Vaughn's payment. Then, trying to seem playful, he pushed off on his desk chair and propelled it close to where Valerie was sitting. A quick glance at that computer revealed she was examining a site devoted to women's shoes.

"Look," he said, "probably you noticed Wallace Vaughn is in the library today. As usual, he's been making a lot of copies. So before I leave I want to let you know where things stand with his payments. I know he's not

18

easy to deal with, but he's also always generous when he comes in here. I put down a few numbers . . ." and he went on to explain what they represented. "Kind of confusing, I know. But are you clear? Any questions?"

"No, I can handle it." Inside his head Daniels echoed but slightly modified her words: I can handle *him*.

"Good," he went on. "Anything else we need to talk about? Am I right you and Janet are switching some hours next week, that's it's on the calendar?

"Right," she answered, sounding bored but also perhaps irritated by an affront to her competence.

He had next-to-no work experience being anyone's "boss" and was aware he could come across as a bit petty playing the role. Nodding at the monitor, he made an effort to lift the tone: "Anything you think would look good on me?"

"I don't see you in stilettos," she countered. "Maybe something not so steep—in price."

From the angle where he sat he could see the clock, almost noon, and the figures of Vaughn and the woman standing together.

Without saying any more to the assistant, he rolled his chair back to the front desk, grabbing the woman's writing as he passed where the papers lay. He was continuing to read when she approached.

"You got a chance to read it?"

"Almost all of it. I'd say you were right about it repeating what you already told me. Even so, there's a bunch of questions that occur to me, about stuff I don't know, things we haven't talked about."

"Oh, I'm sure," she said. "I know it's complicated. But he . . ." she indicated Vaughn, who was standing close

19

behind her, uncharacteristically not talking, "he has some good ideas about what I should do. He offered to take me out to lunch, so that's where we're going now, and he'll explain them. He said he's coming back here this afternoon. Maybe I will too, and see you later?" Her voice rose at the end, shifting into a half-question.

Daniels handed the papers back to her. "I only work till noon," he said softly. "I'm almost finished for today. Valerie" (with a backward nod he indicated the assistant) "will be here. If you want to talk with *me* some more, I'll be in again tomorrow morning. I open the library at 9:00." He felt himself suppressing feelings too mixed to separate.

"You're very good at listening," she said, "and you helped me by doing that—thanks." He watched the two of them leave.

Daniels got to know Duane McKesson when McKesson frequently came to the law library; he was defending himself against a lawsuit that claimed there was an easement across some property he owned in Glen Valley. He had a title map for the parcel which showed no such thing, and he knew well how to do legal research and writing to present his evidence and arguments properly. In fact he lived in an adjacent county, not on the unimproved Glen Valley land, which was about ten miles from the courthouse.

When he arrived or was on his way out, he loved to talk about the case but also much more, in his resonant bass voice that frequently rose into a hearty laugh. He was a horseman, tall and strong, with close-cropped white beard and baseball-style cap bearing the logo of a truck stop or a feedstore. Nearly always there were stories of transporting horses in trailers, then riding into remote forests, mountains, wilderness. A couple of times he'd been on a search-and-rescue team. In Daniels' estimation he was the real-deal Westerner, without making a show of it.

It so happened that he had a record, had been in prison many years earlier for something involving a firearm. Just before Daniels was promoted to head the law library, McKesson applied for a job as an assistant there. The matter came before the Board of Trustees and was summarily shot down by the female judge who was president then, with all the other trustees concurring. Not on my watch, the rejection made clear, is anyone with such a background going to be on the library staff.

21

McKesson strongly believed this treatment was unfair, and he composed a respectful letter to the judge. (He showed it to Daniels.) But nothing changed.

Over time, even though he appeared to have less legal work to do, he would come in just to talk with the librarian, his upbeat mood undimmed.

Of Service

THE FUNDAMENTAL PRINCIPLE of law librarianship was stated in the negative: the librarian should *not* practice law. In concept it made total sense; attorneys, after all, were the ones who'd attended law school, passed the bar exam, and then—with the full backing of the State of California—become fully authorized "officers of the court." Law librarians were not of this ilk; the key word in the name of their profession was "librarian," the highest mission of which was to help people find information. Theirs was honorable work. But Henry Daniels sometimes found himself overly constrained by that definition. Not that he expected to be able to march into court and represent clients. But in wanting his job to have greater meaning, he found himself up against its limitations—he wanted to do more.

His predecessor, in many ways his mentor, seemed to have no difficulty adhering to the fundamental principle. This was ironic in that Edward Donovan in fact *was* an attorney, or at least earlier in his life had been one. He'd retired from the legal profession and then, adding a master's in Library Science to his various other degrees, had taken up the far less stressful (and much less well paid) position of law librarian. His experience enabled him to grasp fully what it meant *not* to practice law, and so he didn't. Thus, presented with the sorts of questions that many patrons of the library tended to ask, he appeared (to Daniels) comfortable not responding with very much in the way of help. This was particularly true if his response would at all approach, to his way of thinking, the "bright line" that marked the statutory boundary between his current and his former line of work.

Having served as Donovan's assistant for seven or eight years, Daniels felt he knew him fairly well, the numerous occasions when both men were in the unbusy library having given Daniels opportunities to talk to Donovan at length about a wide range of subjects. The younger man learned how well read the older one was—he had a special fondness for literature depicting the British Navy—and elicited quite a lot about Donovan's personal history: Bay Area native by birth, given up for adoption and raised in southern Oregon, a resident of San Diego when he practiced law. One of his interests was collectible vehicles; he owned a 1950s-vintage Ford pickup, which he kept in prime condition and displayed at car shows. An entrepreneur, he was the self-published author of a learned tome—an encyclopedia of poison oak—and for several years paid rent on a small office crammed with cartons of the unsold paperback.

Donovan's wife was also a librarian but at the nearby public library, where at the front desk Daniels had become slightly acquainted with her. Ellie was a stern-seeming person with a suffer-no-fools attitude, but select patrons whom she recognized as worthy were permitted to know a woman of extremely high intelligence as well as rapier wit, sometimes even a little warmth.

Very abruptly she was diagnosed with an incurable cancer. After futile surgery, Daniels paid a visit to the hospital. Arriving at the room whose number he'd been given, he found the door open to reveal a poignant sight:

24

the husband's small frame perched awkwardly at the edge of the bed, his left arm uneasily across his wife's shoulders, behind her bandaged head.

Her death triggered a great change in Donovan, a strong urge to retire and move away, perhaps to another state. He recommended to the law library's Board of Trustees that, upon his retirement, Daniels be appointed to succeed him. A much more frequent topic of conversation between the two men then became Donovan's house. Located on a hillside in an attractive neighborhood of Grant City, designed several decades earlier by a renowned architect, it had substantial value; before departing the area, Donovan was determined to hold out for a buyer willing to pay what he believed the house was worth.

There were three or four times when Daniels visited Donovan at the house. On the first, a few days after Ellie died, he delivered some home-cooked food. Later, he was shown the Ford pickup and some features of the distinctive design. At that point Donovan's focus was almost entirely on the large deck behind the house, where seepage from the steep hillside above it, especially during the rainy season, had mandated the need for substantial repair.

After the house finally did sell, Donovan retired. By then he'd met a woman with whom he shared, among other compatible interests, a love of music for string quartet. They later moved further north in California and lived together.

One day Daniels was reading the legal newspaper without great interest when an unfamiliar man crossed the threshold and stopped at the front desk. There was an air about him both nervous and intense, neither of which

25

manner was unsurprising in people who found their way to the law library. His pale eyes were sunk deep in his skull, behind thick glasses. His long hair suggested the fashion of an earlier era, while the partial baldness revealed by its thinning served as evidence of how long ago that era was.

The librarian observed these details only in passing, however, since they didn't much pertain to whatever the man's reasons might be for coming there. "Can I help you?" he asked, with a slight attempt in his voice to put the man at ease.

"Probably not," the man answered, "but I suppose I wouldn't be here if 'no' was the last word on the subject."

The intelligence behind this reply helped raise a logical segué. "And the subject is . . .?"

"Well, of course, that's where things get more complicated."

"You can see," Daniels indicated with a mock-grand sweep of his arm, "I'm not terribly busy. Which means I've got time for you to explain. Can you narrow it down some? I mean, is it a matter of family law? landlord-tenant? restraining order?"

"None of the above," the man said with a slight and slightly bitter laugh. Then, after a pause, "How about road association? Know anything about that?"

"In general I know what a road association is, and I know we've got a book to look into. Do you want to go right to that, or tell me more?"

"First tell, then look."

"Okay," the librarian said. "Would you like to sit down?" He gestured toward the chair close by.

"I guess so, sure, why not?" and before he was even seated he launched into his story. "I've owned my place for thirty-four years. Every single year I paid a fee, to the association, for upkeep of the gravel-and-dirt road that everybody uses. I'm pretty sure the fee was always proportionate to how far up the road your place is. My place is almost halfway up the mountain from Highway 162 to the top of the ridge, which is where it ends.

"In the early days we had work parties and maintained almost the whole thing, lots of people together. It was fun: cleaned out culverts, cleared ditches, filled potholes, smoked pot, drank beer. Later on a guy would bring his backhoe—amazing what a difference *that* thing makes— and not as many people showed up for the work parties. But anyway, now, out of the blue, they send me a huge bill! I know what they say it's for, but even if I thought it was a good thing, which I don't, there's no way I can afford to pay that much."

By the end of his talking he'd become agitated, losing any of the sense of humor he'd displayed before.

Daniels responded moments after recognizing that the man was finished. "Okay, I think I followed most of that. But I've got a couple of questions."

The man said nothing but looked at him as if inviting him to ask.

"'They' is . . . ?"

"The road association. Which is a little bunch of people who, maybe they meet or maybe they don't, I don't really know, but the way the whole subdivision—of the ranch all the land used to be—is set up, some bylaws created the association and said it would be run by a 'governing board.' Yes, that's who 'they' is . . . or are."

"All right," the librarian said, "from the little I know, that setup is pretty standard. But now something has changed. What is 'it'?"

"It." He hesitated and seemed to consider the best definition. "Is a big new development on the last parcel, the top of the ridge, the end of the road. That parcel was always somewhat bigger, it's where the old ranch house was—still *is* really, but it's just been the house of the people who owned the parcel. On just about every other parcel people built their own houses, like I did. Anyway, now, the people at the top want to turn their place into some kind of camp, a 'retreat center' I think they call it. I could care less about that. The point is, because they want to have a lot more people driving all the way up there, year round, and parking, the demands on the road will be much greater. So somehow, and I really don't get the politics, they're trying to squeeze money from all the rest of us, through the road association, to 'improve' the road. I heard the county, as part of granting permission for their 'project,' is going to require them to *pave* the whole thing!"

"Hmmm," the librarian said slowly. "I really appreciate the fact that you came in here, and, like I said, we've got a book that may help. But I'm guessing this library isn't your first stop. Tell me what else you've already done."

The man looked down at his hands, which wrestled each other across his narrow black jeans. "I," he started, but then stopped. There was an uneasy time before he started again. "I haven't been very much . . . connected. I think about talking to other people on the land, I can see that's what I need to be doing, but the truth is, I'm pretty . . . isolated. My wife took off twenty years ago. What I told you I heard about the county? I got that from a guy I ran into at Ray's Market. I know him from those work parties years ago, he lives farther up the road than I do. But I don't know how true what he said is. I don't mean he was lying—I just don't know."

The librarian took all this in before he spoke again. "I'm thinking this would be a good time to take a look at that book. Are you able to be here for a while? I say that because, well—unless you're a lawyer and I'm assuming you're not—you can't *borrow* the book, you need to study it here. But of course you can always come back."

He stood up and walked directly to a set of shelves, each crowded with large books marked by an identical logo on the spine. The man followed him. "All these," Daniels explained, "are published by an outfit called CEB, which stands for Continuing Education of the Bar. That's their logo.

"They're intended mainly for lawyers who need to stay current in their legal specialty. But they can also be useful to non-lawyers—like me and you?—who need to educate themselves. Like this," he said as he reached high and pulled one down. It was one of two volumes titled *Advising California Common-Interest Communities*. "Since all the property owners you mentioned use and have responsibility for the road, they are a 'common-interest community.'

"Actually there are two volumes. The table of contents for both of them is in this first one. Let's take a look at that to find where you want to read. Or, there's an index at the end of Volume Two." He set the book on the glass top of a large wooden table near the shelves, then sat down and flipped it open.

29

Dropping into an adjacent chair, the man said nothing. Daniels, remembering the man's pained self-description, couldn't tell how he was reacting to seeing and hearing about the books. The librarian was concerned he'd overdone his intro and perhaps, without wanting to be, had been condescending. A quick glance at the table of contents suggested that a big theme in Volume One was "governing documents," while Volume Two had a lot about "amending governing documents." He could quickly tell the material applied most widely to condominiums, time-shares, and "gated communities"; nonetheless, he believed they were the right reference to consult in the man's case.

Over his right shoulder he was aware of someone who had entered the library and was waiting near the door. He stood up and asked, "Can I help you?"

It was a young man with elaborate tattoos on both his bare arms. "They told me downstairs I can make copies here." He waved a few pages in one hand.

"Correct. I'll be right with you." But before he moved away he asked the man at the table, "What do you think? Can you start looking into this? I'm gonna help this guy make copies and then I'll come back." He pivoted the CEB book on the glass so that it was directly in front of the man. "Remember, there's an index at the end of Volume Two; you can also go there and try looking up 'road association.'"

Even before he asked the young man for a look at them, he had a strong expectation of what the papers to be copied were. Indeed, they were the three pages of Request to Calendar Case, the form he most frequently encountered for copying, particularly when the patron said "they told me downstairs." He couldn't avoid stereotyping the people who utilized the form, because so often it was for some not-very-substantial reason—forgetting, oversleeping— that the man or woman had missed a hearing and now had to get the case back on the court's calendar.

In such matters it was his habit to proofread the pages before copying them, often finding that the person's residence information was incomplete on page 1; that he or she hadn't written a word in the big box on page 2 to explain the reason for missing the court date; that there was no signature at the end of the form. So sometimes he supplied a pen, told the person to complete the missing parts, and only afterward made the requisite number of copies.

Apart from his initial stereotyping, he in fact got a different feeling about each individual who needed to file a Request to Calendar Case; something about what he sensed in the tattooed man he liked, an air of respectfulness and gratitude.

When Daniels returned to the glass-top table, the first patron's thick glasses were in one hand and he was rubbing his eyes with the other.

"How's it going?" the librarian asked.

The man sat up and put his glasses back on, over eyes that to Daniels looked wet. "Oh, I can see why you thought of this book. It seems to have the right stuff in it. But that's so different from going ahead and doing what I guess needs to be done. Plus my eyes get tired when I try reading anything for very long." With two fingers of each hand he wiped his eyes inside the glasses. "Even if it's a page turner. Which, you probably know, this isn't."

There was that forlorn sense of humor again. "Will you tell me, or show me," Daniels asked, "a little more about what you read?"

The man sighed. "I guess I'd need to find out when this board meets and go to their meeting. To protest. I haven't protested since the Vietnam War."

Daniels felt himself coming up against limits, not only of what he was authorized to do but also of what was logistically possible. The man's situation mirrored his own sense of powerlessness: attention to the news kept him more or less informed, but the world's incessant political/environmental/social/economic tides overwhelmed him.

Contradictorily, one part of him knew that the principles of law librarianship insist that he accept limits, while another part, moved and challenged by the man's story, wanted to become an actor in that story himself. What could *that* possibly mean? That *he* would attend the road association meeting?! Impossible. Yet he felt committed to being of greater service.

Without knowing where he was going, he plunged into nonstop response. "Maybe there are actions short of going to a meeting and speaking at it that would still count as a protest. You could write a letter. Choosing your words and setting them down on paper I think would make you feel you did something. Once you had a letter like that, it would be nagging at you to somehow deliver it. I bet the 'governing documents' contain an address where the association gets its mail. And you either have paperwork with the address on it, or it has to be recorded somewhere—I'd ask at the assessor's office. Do you know where that is? At the post office you send it by 'registered mail—return receipt requested.' People who come in here use that method all the time, to guarantee their legal papers don't just get lost in space. You could drive up to that top parcel, look around—who knows what you'd see or figure out?"

He stopped. In part for the sake of stopping, which by that point seemed essential, in part to gauge the man's reaction.

"How about *you* look in the book?" the man suggested, with, Daniels thought, a faint ray of possibility in his voice. "You didn't have time before you went to help that guy make copies."

"Okay," Daniels said hesitantly. Was he being pulled over the line by the man's inability—or refusal?—to do things for himself? Perhaps the answer was yes, but even so, he believed he would know how and when to stop being pulled. "Let me see where the index takes us on the topic of 'road association.'"

Only the first of the two volumes sat on the table in front of the man, so the librarian stood and reached up to get the second one. In the index's alphabetical order, finding "R" was no problem. But then the listing for "Roads" said only "See Streets and Highways." And when he looked up "Streets and Highways," the subtopics struck him as not leading to information the man needed to find.

"Hmm," he pronounced, "not quite as simple as I thought." He paused, in order to come up with both a different search strategy and words to keep up the man's spirits. "Sometimes this happens. Then it can help to look at it as a kind of game. I don't mean by that to say it's not important. I mean, you have to take a step back and come at things a different way. Finding information can be sort of like solving a puzzle." Playing the game out of his experience at searching, he returned to the table of contents in the first volume and skimmed topics covered in the chapters on "Governing Documents." He didn't say so but wondered whether perhaps the road association was the *only* governing body on the former ranch: if so, how did it operate? who were its members? how were they chosen? There was information in the book about powers, bylaws, meetings. On his own he decided to go first to "powers."

Because the man would need to understand, he explained aloud how, rather than conventional page numbers, the books used an alternate system; for example, "2.15" meant chapter 2, section 15. He turned to the first section on "powers" and then to the man.

"All right," he said firmly. "Time for you to step in again. There's a good chance this will have things you can use. But of course you've got to stretch them to apply to your situation. I know it's not simple. But I get a sense you can do it. You may want to make some notes—if you don't have paper, we've got paper. Or if there's a lot you want to take with you, use the copy machine. See the way the book is made? All the pages are three-hole-punched and held together on this big ring. You can pull the ring apart, lift individual pages out, and copy them. Just make sure to put them back. I'm starting to babble now," he said. "I better shut up."

Daniels returned to his desk near the front door, remembering as he went his confidence-boosting words "I get a sense you can do it." Where did that come from? he wondered. He knew he wanted the man somehow to succeed, even as he realized both of them sorely lacked all the facts of the matter.

Because there were things he needed to do to prepare for the meeting of the law library's Board of Trustees a few days later, he moved to the adjacent desk and logged on to the computer. He reviewed the agenda he had already created and typed the minutes of the last meeting. Then he focused on updating a spreadsheet that would enable the trustees to review income and expenses for each month since the beginning of the fiscal year.

He was double-checking the accuracy of some numbers in the payroll section when, above and beyond the top of the computer monitor, a glimpse of the road-association man standing up caught Daniels' eye. His heart sank: the man was quitting. But a moment later he was beside the front desk, a few pages from the CEB book in his hand. "I've gotta go now, but I plan to come back. These pages are giving me some really good ideas. Could you give me a little more help? I want to use the copy machine."

**   **   **

A woman of striking appearance visited the library half a dozen times. By the colorful floor-length dresses she wore over her long slender body; by the deep-brown color of her skin; and by the accent of her perfectly good English, she was African, it seemed to Daniels. The curving lines of her eyes, nose, and mouth added to a certain elegance. Her hair was covered entirely by a loose headscarf gathered into a very large sack behind her neck. This the librarian recognized as garb worn by Rastafarians, the Jamaicans who savor ganja and move rhythmically to reggae music; inside the sack, he assumed, was a mass of "dreads," long locks of hair tightly curled and ironed. Yet, even though his assumption ventured beyond what he knew for sure, he thought she was not from Jamaica but Africa.

Each time she came to the library she was accompanied by three children. The energy and curiosity in them, especially the two older ones, a boy and a girl, was barely containable. They swarmed around the computer desks wanting to touch anything and everything, but were kept distracted, at least temporarily, by the scratch paper and pencils and pens she and Daniels put in their hands. The youngest was still a toddler, and her mother needed to give her a different kind of attention. All the while the woman attempted to deal with her legal business, which presumably had to be conducted over a long period of time, hence her repeated visits. Except for access to a computer she needed no help, so the librarian never learned what the business was. Nevertheless, the two of

36

them made small talk and built a very slight acquaintance over the course of the many months. He was struck by her exotic beauty and unflappable motherhood; she appreciated his welcome.

The Activist

ONE DAY A DIMINUTIVE WOMAN strode across the threshold and announced to Henry Daniels, "I need a computer."

It so happened that one of two computers reserved for the public was already in use, by one of the library's non-attorney regulars. Because the third computer was reserved for library staff, this meant only one was available for the woman, and Daniels quickly guided her to it.

"You seem to know what you're doing," he commented quietly. "Is there anything I can help you with?"

"I need to type a letter that I've already mostly written in longhand," she explained. "It needs to be on computer so I can send it as email to the *Fort Pierce Press-Enterprise*, which has a deadline this afternoon. When the letter is finished, I will require your assistance so I can send it."

"All right."

"Let's see," she went on, barely stopping to hear, "how do I type the letter?"

"You . . . don't know how to type?" he ventured.

"No, of course I know that," she snapped. "How do I do it here?"

Daniels reached for the mouse and brought up a blank word-processing page. "Go ahead and type it on there. Then when you're done let me know, and I can help you send it." As an afterthought, he inquired, "You have the email address?" She was already engaged in typing and just nodded sharply.

Glancing before he moved away, the librarian noted a few details of her appearance. On top of her dark wiry hair at a stylish angle sat a black beret. The skin of her face was nut-brown and weathered, almost as much by being outside, he guessed, as by age. A loose black wool dress entirely covered her, down to the workboots on her very small feet, except for the wrinkled fingers of both her hands, which extended to the keyboard. Wrapped loosely around her neck was a long red scarf.

His glance also caught her name, on a business card stapled to the notebook she put beside the computer. He realized he knew her, by reputation anyway, as a frequently published writer of letters to editors as well as caller to talk shows on KMZT, Manzanita County's public radio station. He remembered her outspokenness, her irreducible outrage no matter what the topic. Now he savored the opportunity to match a face with that name.

Because at the time he had so little else to do, it would be inaccurate to say he "busied" himself while she typed. A familiar attorney came in and nodded to Daniels, but, needing no assistance, went directly to the rear of the library. Two women, definitely not attorneys (as he felt sure by their clothes and hairstyles), entered and asked for help making copies. The material was handwritten on both sides of four rumpled pages. One of the two seemed to be there in support of the other, though he couldn't eavesdrop adequately to be sure; an intriguing air surrounded the women, but neither did they volunteer any information nor was he nosy enough to seek it.

After they paid for the copies and left, he sat idle again at the front desk. He wondered when the woman at the computer would be finished typing her letter. He also wondered, with wholly internal amusement, whether he should, or would, broach to her the fact that he recognized her name. Revealing that fact would probably open a more complex exchange between them; it might even flatter her. Yet it was possible she'd interpret it as a kind of trespass, a going where he didn't belong. In light of the too-familiar situation of his idleness, he knew he preferred the former. But he could see he'd also need to accept the latter if that's what transpired. His imagining of whatever the continuation of their encounter might be was colored further by the way she'd spoken and acted toward him.

He'd stirred himself out of this reverie and begun flipping through a folder pertaining to workers' compensation insurance (on a paper inside the folder were the details of a small task that was his responsibility) when the woman's voice stated, for anyone to hear, "I'm ready to send now."

It was obvious to Daniels that he was the intended recipient of those words, but he was tempted to react with less than all-out speed. Soon enough, though, without her having to repeat herself, he was standing beside and above her. A very quick look at the monitor captured multiple uses in the letter of the word "Caltrans" (the corporate-style name of the California Department of Transportation) and the phrase "Johnsville bypass." It came as absolutely no surprise to the librarian that the woman would have strong views about these two; construction of the latter by the former was a matter of intense controversy, by no

40

means restricted to residents of Johnsville, a town about twenty miles north of Grant City.

"Ah," he said, "Johnsville bypass."

"Yes," she responded. "An abomination. A catastrophe." It was the same tone of voice he remembered from the radio, gaining force by being spoken beside him.

Daniels was very familiar with the numerous issues— economic, environmental, even archaeological— surrounding construction of the massive new highway. "You oppose it," he said, not inflecting his words as a question.

"Obviously. Don't you?" She didn't wait for him to answer. "There are a great many more reasons than I had time to put into this letter. So it's mainly about a demonstration this Sunday. One woman is going to chain herself to a concrete mixer. I haven't decided yet whether to join her. But I'll be there, and at the very least I can help with publicity."

An image of an activist dwarfed by massive machinery but tied to it by a chain arose in Daniels' mind. Would she also be chained to the other protestors, in solidarity? How would they get to the mixer? It had to be on the other side of a spiky fence, maybe many fences. On a Sunday, would anyone from Caltrans be there? Getting paid overtime? The Highway Patrol. Almost certainly Johnsville police. His mind was generating these kinds of image, but when he spoke it was simply to ask, "You said you have the email address?"

"I do."

"Is there a person you're sending the letter to? That may not be absolutely necessary, but if you have one, I'll use it. And do you want a copy printed out? For you to keep? Let me sit there, will you please?"

They traded places. Because she evidently was not a computer user, he was unsure how much of the process she needed, or wanted, to know. She opened her notebook and found a page where the address and the editor's name were written.

"I was on the phone with him before I came in here. He said their deadline is usually ten o'clock but that he'd give me until noon to get my letter to him. Otherwise it won't be in the paper until their issue of next week—a waste, since the demo will be over."

Daniels knew he himself was no great whiz on computers and had actually never done what she wanted. Still, he had a logical sense of how to proceed and did so, using the library's own email account as the vehicle for delivering her letter. It occurred to him that he was overstepping the limit of what a law librarian should properly do, but he was untroubled because he judged it merely as helping a patron.

"How will I know they got it?" she asked. "That's important—I told you."

"I'll ask him to reply, confirming it got there. But it seems to me that *you*'ll need to wait here, since the reply will come to the library's email account, which I can check every few minutes." He looked up and caught an expression of what he interpreted as annoyance or impatience flash across her face.

"I live far out of town," she began, as if obliged against her will to explain herself, "and when I come in I've got a long list of things to do. This was at the top of my list. But

I didn't expect to have to 'hang out' here. I've got many other things."

"I hear you. I don't know what else to tell you."

She didn't say another word until she jumped in with "You haven't even sent it yet, am I right? Do *that* anyway."

She was correct. With a few clicks on the keyboard and passes with the mouse, he completed the job. "Done—first things first. Now it's on its way."

Neither of them said anything for a few moments. Then, with a note of triumph she said, "I suppose it got there in an instant. Isn't that how email works? What about calling now? You could ask if he got it."

Me? he thought. He felt pressured by her and was starting to resent it. But the words he spoke didn't show those feelings: "*You* could call him. You said you did that before."

"I came into town with a friend with a cell phone. Now she's off somewhere else. I don't have one."

Daniels realized that in the pattern of their exchange it was his turn to say something and within his power to steer the conversation. But he found himself in an odd bind: his good intentions clashed with the very different ones of a patron who barely noticed them. He realized he wanted to continue assisting her but simultaneously maintain some intangible degree of integrity. A part of him was insistent on confronting the woman about her attitude, while another part was very reluctant to respond to *any* patron in such a manner. As these thoughts contended within him, he remained silent.

Finally, choosing a way forward, he said, "I guess he won't be getting a call right away then. I'll let you use the library's phone in a little while. In the meantime, believe it or not, you're not the only thing going on." (He was aware as he said this last line that it wasn't altogether true.) "If you'll excuse me, I want to sit at that computer." With his head he indicated the one reserved for library business. Then he stood and moved to it, which forced her to take a step back. As he passed in front of her, he couldn't tell whether she was fuming over his non-compliance.

"How long will this be?" she asked very soon, in a tone of voice echoing the expressions he thought he'd read on her face. "I told you I'm busy."

"Let me ask *you* something, Pamela. Is this always the way you get what you want?"

She was taken aback at his use of her name. "How do you know—?"

"Who you are. Your card on the front of your notebook. But I've seen it in print lots of times before now. And I even recognize your voice, from all the calls you make to 'The Discussion.'"

A smile flashed coldly across her features. "They don't give me enough time."

"'Time.'" He mocked her a little: "That's a key word for you today."

"Me?! It's not about me! It's critically important for the planet! How much *time* do we *all* have left?!"

He considered her question unanswerable yet felt chastened by her intensity. "That's not one I want to argue," he said. "I respect what you're doing. And I'm trying to help. Now give me a few minutes, then one of us can call that editor. If you like, I'll show you how to use the computer while you're waiting, to find information you might use later."

44

"No, never mind," she replied, in a quite different tone he couldn't interpret. She sat down in the computer chair, apparently accepting the wait.

Daniels opened the library-business computer and, uncommitted to any particular work to perform there, reflexively clicked on the library's email account. There were usually new messages to view, and at a minimum it was productive to delete the unimportant ones. The "Inbox" displayed eight or ten new messages. He rapidly put a check mark in the box beside five of them, then clicked "Delete." The others could wait for later. He had a more interesting idea: he clicked on the "Sent" folder and could see immediately that the most recently sent message was the woman's letter. The fact it appeared on that list was confirmation her letter had indeed been sent (which was good to know). If he opened it, he could read what it said. Should he? With nearly no hesitation he told himself not to.

He looked briefly in the direction of the woman. The monitor on the desk in front of her blocked his view of her face, but he could tell by the position of her feet that she was turned 90° away from it. Her hands, uncharacter-istically, were idle in her lap. He had a strong sense that some change had come over her. Was it possible she might be reacting, as had he, to their exchange of just a few moments ago?

It occurred to him to send an email to the newspaper editor, requesting assurance that the letter would run. But making a phone call actually seemed a better strategy, because then there would be no need to wait for a reply. So Daniels admitted to himself he was playing a mind game by making Pamela wait. Still, he couldn't ignore

45

what in her behavior had led him to play the game. He wanted to maintain his fundamental commitment to patrons of the library, but there was no guarantee every transaction would stick to his private "rules" of behavior.

As he stood up, her face came into view over the top of the monitor. "I see by checking our email account that your letter has been sent. Would you like to call now?" He reached for the cordless phone.

"Yes," she answered, and, after a pause, added, "thank you."

He handed her the phone and then walked away toward the rear of the library, partly to give her some privacy but also to shield his reaction to her sudden politeness. From a table he picked up the latest issue of the legal newspaper to which the library subscribed and brought it with him when he returned to the front desk. She was on her feet and finished with her call. She handed him the phone, which he replaced on its stand. "How'd it go?" he asked.

"Just fine," she answered. "He needed to go to his computer to find my . . . our . . . message/letter/whatever. So I waited while he did that, and then he told me it will run tomorrow."

"I'm glad that worked out," Daniels said.

As she prepared to leave, for a moment they were in positions to look more fully at each other. Daniels observed a brightness in her dark brown eyes. Perhaps, he thought, the woman—Pamela—was seeing something in him she hadn't seen before.

He hesitated before speaking. "Something I've been wondering. Maybe there's no answer, or no simple one: how will you decide whether to join that protest?"

"Are *you* thinking of protesting, too?"

"No," he laughed, mocking himself: "law librarians aren't allowed. And I can 'read all about it' later. But *you* have a reputation preceding you."

Now she was the one who hesitated. "It all depends—of course. On the weather, the scene, the 'vibe.' I'm expecting my son to come from Seattle and visit, but at this point I don't know whether he'll get here Saturday, Sunday, or even Monday. Do I want him to have to find me in jail? And my garden: I've got vegetable starts in the ground. Who's going to tend to them if not me? Or are those things just selfish compared to this disgusting bypass?" She wound the red scarf once more around her neck. "You may be surprised to hear me say it, but I really don't have all the answers."

One semi-regular visitor was a young attorney whose parents Henry Daniels had known for thirty-five years. (The librarian was a guest at Zachary's wedding.) When he returned to Grant City after college and several years elsewhere, he worked for a time in a county department. But then he decided to go to law school and successfully switched careers. After that, while there were professional reasons bringing him to the courthouse and though he usually had no business to conduct in the law library, Zachary clearly enjoyed stopping there, too. Daniels was always pleased to see him.

Their conversation was predominantly about sports, a subject very familiar to both but about which the attorney was extraordinarily knowledgeable. For any item Daniels might bring up about the San Francisco 49ers, for example, Zachary responded with much more and deeper information, about the team, its individual players, and the rest of the NFL. In baseball, for reasons he once explained, he was an avid Baltimore Orioles fan. Across the board he had no shortage of very confident opinions and predictions. Daniels learned from all these exchanges, but more notably he was impressed by the younger man's sharp intelligence and worldly humor. Zachary was no longer a kid.

Six or eight years after the wedding, the librarian became aware of drastic change in Zachary's circumstances. Although he and his wife already had two young children, her overzealous devotion to a fitness cult of some kind broke the marriage apart (as Daniels heard from various sources, including the parents). Before long the still-young attorney was living in a much smaller house, a part-time single father trying to manage a difficult life.

**   **   **

An attorney with a British accent sometimes had business to conduct in the law library, and he was always quite friendly toward Daniels on those occasions. But when their paths crossed elsewhere in the courthouse, the lawyer never gave the slightest indication of knowing the librarian. Daniels tried to shrug off these non-encounters but felt stung by them even so. Despite the word "city" in its name, the county seat was small-town enough that total strangers often nodded to one another on its sidewalks, even said hello. He hated being ignored.

A Meeting of the Board

THE STATUTES of the State of California were divided into 29 separate codes: the Code of Civil Procedure, the Tax and Revenue Code, the Penal Code, and 26 more. A sequence in the Business and Professions Code very precisely defined the law library. It was something of an orphan—not part of the court system, not part of any state agency, not part of county government. Yet there, in black and white, was its mandate: in each of the 58 counties there *shall* be one.

Near the beginning of the sequence one statute dictated the membership of a law library's Board of Trustees. For a tiny-population county, such as Alpine or Modoc, the number of members required to be on the Board was proportionately very small. Manzanita County, with its quite small but not tiny population (spread across a vast land area), was nevertheless large enough to be in the same category as California's far more populous counties. This required its Board to have seven trustees.

The code specified that one trustee was to be appointed by the county's Board of Supervisors. Another was to be appointed by the chairman (update: "chairperson") of the Board of Supervisors, a rule that doubled the influence of that local body. The other five were to be judges of the Superior Court in the county; or, in lieu of them or some of them, local attorneys whom the judges were to appoint.

As law librarian Daniels was not a member of the Board but served as its secretary, taking minutes at the meetings,

50

which were supposed to happen once a month. One of his tasks was to prepare a packet in advance of them, and, since he was the one who knew most about the library's business, he found he did most of the talking at them. This felt uncomfortable: not a lawyer, certainly not a judge, he couldn't help but feel inferior to the trustees. He doubted such a comparison ever crossed any of their minds and that, if asked, they'd praise him. *So what*, his inner voice insisted: *You're not one of them.*

Perhaps it was his characteristic pessimism, but when Daniels studied the spreadsheet numbers he included in the packet, it was his strong conviction that sooner or later the library would run out of money. Month after month after month, notification from the state regarding how much "filing-fee revenue" was to be deposited in the library's account glared with numbers he knew couldn't indefinitely sustain the tiny operation.. Yet, once when he shared this assessment with the Board, Daniels, according to one judge, was the chicken who shouted "the sky is falling." The other trustees chuckled at the caricature, which proved to have great staying power.

It wasn't rare that three or fewer trustees would show up for a meeting, which meant there was no quorum, and so the meeting wasn't official. What this typically did was create a brief chance for the ones who did show to chat. Daniels realized that membership on this board wasn't prestigious for any of the trustees and that all of them were far busier people than he was. Still, considering what he'd put into readying the packet and himself, these times to him were washouts.

Not infrequently someone would enter the law library and ask how to challenge a judge. This question sometimes came prior to a hearing or other court appearance, but more often the person asking it was furious about a decision just rendered. Convinced that the judge was absolutely in the wrong, the patron wanted to learn what procedures existed, what rights he or she had to insist that someone else be put on the bench.

Because the question had arisen so often in the past, Daniels knew exactly where to go. A massive reference set titled *California Forms of Pleading and Practice* filled floor-to-ceiling shelves on the back wall of the library. Its topics were organized in alphabetical order, and he'd reach directly for the volume dealing with "Judges"; it in turn was subdivided into chapters on all sorts of matters, from the election of judges to their permanent removal from the bench to one devoted to "recusal." The last was the technical term for the outcome the patron sought: either because a judge decided to recuse him- or herself or, more likely, because under state law the particulars of a case insisted the judge step aside.

Daniels kept to himself his opinion that, for a more or less ordinary plaintiff or defendant, recusal was very much a long shot. Instead, he felt he'd done his duty by guiding a dissatisfied patron to the appropriate chapter and leaving him or her to study the lay of the law. If the person seemed especially overwhelmed by the reference material, the librarian would ask if he could be of further assistance. And if the person was open to it, he'd help decipher the text (sometimes again wondering where the "bright line" lay).

A challenging situation arose when the librarian learned that a certain patron wanted to challenge a judge who sat on the Board. It so happened that Daniels knew the man slightly because he was a regular who prepared for his continual forays into court by making frequent and extensive use of the library. The man seemed intelligent, apparently confident enough in his own knowledge of legal research and writing that he never requested help doing them. Thus Daniels was not much familiar with details of the battle the man was waging. Part of his use of the library, however, was making copies of motions and other paperwork, and it was from seeing the headings on these that the librarian gained his very limited knowledge: most of them named high officials of the state, such as the Governor, as defendants.

Daniels perceived intensity within the stockily built man, dark and barely suppressed anger bordering on desperation. A choleric complexion beneath incompletely brushed hair seemed further evidence of that inner turbulence. Denim workshirt on a powerful upper body, dark-green cargo shorts year round, and tall laced boots were his everyday costume. He was invariably gruff, offering the librarian no more than a curt nod when he crossed the threshold. Even with these unappealing traits, however, perhaps *because* the man was so evidently an outsider to the so-called "justice system," Daniels felt a degree of sympathy for him.

One morning the patron burst into the library quite clearly angrier even than usual. He was muttering to himself about Judge Morrison, who was currently presiding in Courtroom E; she had just ruled against one of his motions, and he was intent on challenging her. Because he seemed to know how to locate everything he needed,

Daniels, at the front desk, was surprised when he blurted out, "I need to know about recusal. Where's that?"

As the man set his briefcase down beside the computer where he routinely worked, then strode toward the rear of the library, Daniels was right behind him. From the shelves that contained *California Forms of Pleading and Practice*, the librarian brought down the "Judges" volume, then turning it slightly on its side found the tab marked "Recusal." He opened the volume to that chapter, found the pages marked "Contents," and said, "I suggest you skim these to look for what you want."

As he handed the big blue binder to the man, who immediately sat down with it at the table in front of the shelves, it occurred to Daniels that the table was the site of the Board meetings and that Judge Morrison usually sat in that same chair.

"She's so full of shit," the man fumed. "I can't believe she keeps fucking me over."

No one else was in the library at the time, so the librarian chose not to make the profanity an issue. If there had been, Daniels knew he'd have had to caution him. Instead, he understood it as heat from a cauldron inside the man. "Anything you want to talk about?"

"What could *you* do about it anyway?" the man snapped back. "You're just part of all the bullshit in this county."

"Okay, okay," Daniels responded this time. "I think I've heard enough . . ."

"Oh, it's not you—*she* just keeps nitpicking me to death. This time it was because the format on the cover page had one meaningless mistake in it. I know for a fact she overlooks stuff like that for other people who represent themselves around here. She's really got it in for me."

54

"I hear different things about different judges," the librarian said, and right away, because it was so vapid, wished he hadn't.

"What do you hear about her?"

"Nothing I could put in one simple label. She's smart. She's efficient. She works hard. And in fact she's on the Board of Trustees of this place."

The man hesitated before he spoke again. "Oh, now I get it. Of course you're not going to cross her. She's your boss."

"I wouldn't put it that way at all. Yes, I pay attention to her, but no, she doesn't tell me what to do."

A woman had entered the library and was standing near the front. Daniels walked away in her direction and left the man to study "Recusal." He and the woman knew each other slightly from her previous visits to the library. She worked for an attorney, sometimes coming in to do research, other times, as on this day, just for copies. "Three of each page," she said. The two of them made small talk as he completed the copy job and then collected payment for it. All the while, beneath the surface of their pleasant exchange, he was processing the man's comments.

He remained at the front desk after she left, at first to record the little transaction, but then to think more about the judge. Naturally, his relations with the trustees differed according to the individual, but still some things could be said about dealing with the group as a whole. His attitude toward their profession led him, despite the superficially inclusive air at the Board meetings, to feel alienated. Their solidarity was of an elite, while he saw himself in a lower caste. He thought the man's idea that Daniels' relation to them was one of employee to employer was off the mark.

Or was it? Month in, month out, the "actions" of the Board at its meetings were so inconsequential as to render any idea of them as his "boss" silly. He believed one reason he had gravitated to this job, as with other work situations in his past, was that primarily he supervised himself. Still, he couldn't entirely dismiss the notion that he'd internalized their trusteeship and was doing what he was told without any of them needing to say anything. Preparing the packet: were all the pains he took a slavish desire to please?

The angry man was named Jonathan Stryker, which Daniels first learned by glancing at his paperwork, but then too because Stryker accumulated a considerable tab of IOUs for copies. The size of the debt was larger than Daniels was typically comfortable allowing anyone, but because Stryker always eventually had the cash necessary to pay it all off, Daniels kept extending him this form of credit.

Besides the business with the IOUs, there was another, stranger aspect of Stryker's use of the library that ran counter to its regular mode of operation. This was the fact that Stryker saved a very large number of documents on "his" computer, often leaving them on the desktop, which consequently looked far more crowded than the desktops of the other two computers. Once Daniels sat at that one when Stryker wasn't around; clicking the mouse on items extraneous to the library's basic display, he could see there were numerous items gathered from a variety of websites.

He followed this up the next day by speaking to Stryker about it: "I see you're keeping a lot of things on the desktop that really shouldn't be there."

"Like what?"

"I'm sure you know what. Different downloads from the Internet."

"So you've been reading my stuff?" His tone was in equal parts offended and hostile.

"The last thing I want to do is to be 'looking over your shoulder'—I know it's private and none of my business. But *you* don't seem to care that all of it's right out where anyone can read it. And besides, the library discourages people from saving their own things to the computers."

Stryker looked disgusted but didn't say anything.

"I'm asking you to deal with this. At the least you could put everything that's yours in one folder. I suppose that folder could stay on the desktop. Or there must be a way to keep the folder on the computer somewhere else but take it off the desktop. I'd have to play around to figure out how to do that, which I'd be glad to do. The point is, you've been doing something you're not supposed to, and now I'm . . ." he hesitated as he slowly chose the words "doing my job."

Two days later Daniels checked, and nothing on the crowded desktop had changed.

Even with these annoyances considered, Stryker was an example of a certain category of patron: a person not particularly likable but whom, Daniels firmly believed, the library was intended to help. The sheer fact that Stryker made such extensive use of the place was a good thing, and Daniels was reluctant to do anything, such as insisting on immediate payment for copies, to deter him from trusting that its resources were available to him. In this narrow sense, whether he was being treated justly by the court system or not didn't matter. Stryker was in fact right when he said Daniels could do nothing beyond the library, but at

57

least within its confines the librarian could assure fair treatment for everyone who entered it.

Following the departure of the woman who came in for copies, and knowing Stryker's habit of conducting his business by himself, Daniels felt no need to follow up on their previous interaction and was inclined not to. As abstract as the title *California Forms of Pleading and Practice* sounded, it really did contain very concrete explanations and guidelines, written for attorneys but understandable by laypeople, for using state law to accomplish a myriad of legal objectives. Daniels in the past had frequently seen Stryker seated at that same table, no doubt consulting it and other reference works in the course of drafting his motions. Now, before long, Stryker returned to "his" computer and set the opened "Judges" volume beside the monitor.

Stryker's habit was to work intently for several hours, then disappear, for lunch or who knew where, and return the next morning. After about an hour, he unexpectedly came to the front desk, where Daniels sat minimally occupied.

"How often does your Board meet?" Stryker asked him.

"Usually the last Friday of the month, at noon."

"Are the meetings open to the public?"

"Yep. Anyone can attend."

"If you're not on that Board, are you allowed to speak?"

"Yes. It's part of what 'open to the public' means."

There was an interval of silence, neither man choosing to say more. But then Daniels spoke again: "You're thinking of coming to one?"

"Obviously." His tone in saying that one word was deeply disparaging, and Daniels had to work to separate himself from the actual target of Stryker's putdown, which he speculated was the judge, the Board, or the system altogether. No matter what effort he made, he felt himself caught in the crosscurrents of the situation, particularly if Stryker were to follow through on his idea and show up at a meeting.

Lying flat on top of the front desk was a large calendar, sparsely filled with information pertaining to the month. Sure enough, in the square for the last Friday was written "Bd mtg." It was ten days away. Stryker noticed it and asked Daniels, "So that's the next one? the 27th?"

"Correct." Knowing that the standard format of the Board agenda included "Public Comment," Daniels debated whether to bring it up. Then he went ahead and told Stryker, "If you want, I can put you on their agenda. There's a time for 'Public Comment'."

"Nah. I'm not even sure I want to be there."

Daniels wasn't sure whether their conversation was over. He could have continued by asking whether the "Judges" material was useful, but he didn't. In his gruff manner, Stryker turned and walked away.

The librarian had already drafted an agenda, one of several items in the packet, for the next meeting. He kept it very brief, as usual imitating the format of sessions past. It was a document on the library's computer, easily able to be modified and typically not printed until the day before the meeting, with a copy for each trustee. An accompanying page of the packet titled "Librarian's Report" was the section where he went into much greater detail about current library business, things he determined the Board needed to know. At the top of the page was a listing of the previous six-months' filing-fee revenue, month by month; he wanted the members to see what he saw there, namely, the dreary trend of numbers too low to sustain the operation as its costs, above all for subscriptions, inexorably rose.

The body of the "Librarian's Report" was the part of the packet on which Daniels spent the most time. Sometimes this was because an item of business was in progress and he wanted to provide the Board with the latest report on it, so he kept updating the news. In other cases he was continuously editing himself, striving to "speak" to the trustees as articulately as he could. With regard to this latter effort he assumed they read carefully; in light of the fact that the meetings took just a few minutes of their time each month, though, he knew his assumption wasn't reasonable. Still, his habit persisted.

The prospect of Stryker appearing on the 27th was radical in contrast with the relaxed, clubby nature of the typical meeting. The librarian sought refuge from what might conceivably be a storm by focusing on the fact that it wouldn't be—how could it be?—about Daniels himself.

On the days that followed and into the week of the meeting, Stryker continued to use the library, crossing the threshold with a surly nod, then proceeding to the computer he always used. Along with occasionally helping patrons at the copy machine or supplying relatively simple answers to questions others asked, Daniels continued to create the packet. Writing the minutes of the previous meeting was easy because so little had happened at it. There undoubtedly needed to be a record of the library's past, but he couldn't recall himself or anyone else ever needing to look anything up in the gray binder of old minutes. He

60

also kept entering numbers and double-checking them on the computer spreadsheet, the fourth section of the packet. His efforts here were aimed at accurately presenting a YTD (year-to-date) number that summarized the entire financial position of the library. Both analogous to and directly influenced by the filing-fee revenue, this number was always negative.

As of the middle of the morning on the 27th, he'd heard nothing more from Stryker, who also hadn't come into the library so far that day. As he printed out and assembled a finished packet for each trustee, he wondered whether to make an extra for the possible guest, in order that Stryker would be able to read what the members were reading. Around 11:40 Daniels went to the rear of the library and pulled the table slightly away from its normal position, toward the bookshelves, so there would be room around it for seven wooden armchairs, which he maneuvered into comfortable position, plus one for himself. Another table of identical size sat parallel to the one where the Board would sit; should Stryker show up, Daniels envisioned directing him to sit there.

The librarian always experienced a degree of anxiety in advance of the gathering of the Board. While the agenda for the meeting contained nothing out of the ordinary nor did the other components of the packet, this knowledge wasn't enough to put him at ease. The possibility of Stryker's appearing of course intensified how he felt.

He left all but one of the packets on the table; the trustees as they arrived typically headed there, took one, and, if they weren't conversing with one another, began looking over the pages. The one set he took back with him to the front desk. This was tentatively to give to the Board president, who usually arrived a few minutes ahead of the others and stood across the front desk from Daniels, half-studying the information and half-talking with the librarian about it or other matters. The president, a judge, was the one who had first teased Daniels about his worry that "the sky is falling." The librarian's general opinion of the legal profession notwithstanding, Daniels genuinely admired this man's intelligence, enjoyed his wit, and appreciated his warmth.

At about 11:55, in came a long-time member of the Board, Richard Brock, a man of wiry build who, Daniels knew, specialized in probate law. He nodded to the librarian and proceeded to the table in the back. A minute later, sure enough the Board president entered. "Henry," he said, extending his hand across the table and giving Daniels' a brisk shake, "how *are* you today?"

"Doing well enough, Marty," he answered. (In other settings, "Judge" or even "Your Honor" would have been deemed appropriate, but, according to subtle courthouse protocols as he understood them, Daniels was confident that first-name basis here was fine.)

"I know of two members who won't be able to make it today," the judge said respectfully, "and in fact *I* have another meeting at 12:30. So I hope this can be quick."

"I don't know, Judge," Daniels responded. "You all were supposed to be hearing oral arguments today." In the same instant he both masked his disappointment that there might not be a quorum and silently congratulated his own quick wit. "But I'll see what I can do." After a moment during which the judge glanced at the packet, Daniels added, "It shouldn't take long."

Next to cross the threshold was the assistant who worked Friday afternoons; she would be at the front desk while Daniels was at the meeting. The judge gave her a friendly hello before moving to the table in the rear. The librarian, who enjoyed a mildly joking relationship with Ruth, the assistant, only had time on this busy day to transmit to her a few bits of current business. During those moments two more trustees arrived, one of whom was Judge Morrison.

At 12:05, no other trustees (or members of the public) having appeared, Daniels walked back to the table knowing that the four already present comprised a quorum and that the meeting should therefore begin. His arrival and the president's rapid call to order were followed by routine approval of the minutes: the noncontroversial vote was unanimous.

"Anything in your report we should pay special attention to, Henry?"

"Well," Daniels responded, "the filing-fee trend continues. I've mentioned before that the network of all the county law librarians in the state is trying to mount a campaign to influence the legislature, to help solve this problem. As you directed me to do at your last meeting, I drafted letters to our representatives and the governor— basically I just followed a form letter from the network— and plugged in numbers specific to the situation in this county. Those letters are ready for you as Board president to sign, and I'll send them. Plus of course everyone is welcome to review them."

"How much chance do you think there is of us getting more money?" asked Richard Brock.

"Honestly, not much," said Daniels. "It just doesn't seem law libraries are on anyone's radar in Sacramento. And there's so much competition for funding—of everything."

At that moment a fifth trustee walked briskly into the library and proceeded to join the meeting. This was Jason Keyes, an attorney who specialized in family law. "Sorry I'm late, everybody, I was in court. I knew the judge was going to call a break for lunch but there was no telling when." The others slightly shifted their chairs to make room for him, and a few moments of camaraderie among them ensued. Daniels added the initials JK to the scant notes he was taking, which would later become minutes.

Then, behind him and to his right, the librarian sensed someone else entering. He heard the low pitch of a man's voice and the higher one of Ruth's. Daniels had intended, in his own brief exchange with her, to inform her of the possibility of Stryker's attending the meeting, but in the brief commotion around noon he had failed to do so. Now in a flash he imagined she was making an effort to impede Stryker's advance and that Stryker was having none of it. Imagining gave way even faster to the reality of Stryker standing in the rear of the library. Daniels thought Judge Morrison was shifting slightly in her chair, but then he acknowledged that this could have been his imagination. He stood up and moved toward Stryker, simultaneously pulling a chair out from the adjacent table and handing him a packet. "This is what they're all working from," he said. "I was going over some points on the second page, the 'Librarian's Report.'"

Daniels returned to his chair and announced to the trustees, "This man is Jonathan Stryker, who uses the

64

library quite frequently. He expressed an interest in attending a Board meeting, and I told him your meetings are open to the public." Stryker's head was down, apparently reading the packet. Daniels couldn't gauge whether his unexpected presence made the Board at all uncomfortable.

"So where were we, Henry?" the president asked. "You remember I told you I've got another meeting at 12:30."

"Right. If you look at the spreadsheet, you'll recall that I consider the year-to-date number at the lower left the best summary of how we're doing. You can see it's in negative territory, as it has been, and next month will almost certainly be more of the same because some big quarterly bills have to be paid then. You've heard me point out that the year-to-date is closely tied to the filing-fee numbers, which are shown as monthly income across the top of the spreadsheet. I'd be glad to answer any questions, but I think you get the picture."

He waited for any questions but there appeared to be none, so he added, "I've told you before, I'm convinced you need to not renew some of the more expensive subscriptions, as a way of cutting costs. But the time to do that isn't until their renewal dates, so I guess you don't have to discuss it today."

"How far off are those renewal dates?" Jason Keyes asked. "I want to know because I'm going to be out of town the last Friday of next month, and maybe we don't need to meet until two months from now."

"As far as the renewal dates are concerned, you could wait that long," Daniels said. "At this point I don't really know what other business you'll have if you meet in one month."

65

"What about other people?" Keyes asked the rest of the members. "Anybody object to putting it off?"

Nobody argued strenuously against skipping a month, and the president, bringing up the calendar on his tablet, made it official: "Two months from now the last Friday is on the 29th. So we'll meet then at noon. Henry, please email the members who are absent so they'll know."

"I've got a question," came a voice from the adjacent table. Two members, one the Board president, had been sitting with their backs to Stryker, and they now half-turned to face him.

"Yes?" replied the president. His tone was polite but a little impatient.

"What is this—some kind of joke? You call this a meeting? The main action you took was a postponement! What kind of rinky-dink is that?"

"You said you had a question," the president said, "but it sounded to me like just your opinion. It's true our meetings are 'open to the public,' but that doesn't mean 'open to abuse from the public.'"

The trustees were rising from their chairs, preparing to leave.

Richard Brock suddenly spoke to Stryker. "I've seen you in here quite a few times before, when I've come to look things up. It seems you're always at that same computer, always with piles of paper and books around you."

The trustee who had entered the library at the same time as Judge Morrison was a young female attorney who worked extra hard to mix private practice with her responsibilities as a mother. Occasionally, Daniels recalled, she'd missed meetings because she didn't have

66

child care. Now she spoke emphatically to Stryker: "I've seen you, too. It's one thing to use the law library, but something very different to use it as your office. We have a policy about that. This is not a place to hang out or conduct your personal business."

Stryker glowered but said nothing in response. The meeting having concluded, each member was still in a phase of exit. But all of them also were arrested by the fierceness of the exchange with their "guest." The president, in the midst of replacing his tablet in his briefcase, asked Daniels, "What is our policy, Henry?"

The librarian answered, "The policy we have is about getting off a computer if someone else is waiting to use it. If that's the case, the person on the computer is told to get off it within ten minutes."

"It doesn't specifically say anything about using the library as an office then?" the younger attorney wanted to know.

"Not that I'm aware of," Daniels said.

"Well, I'd like there to be something stronger than what Henry says we've got," said Jason Keyes. "I've seen this guy in here too."

The thought occurred to Daniels that the office concept might be difficult to define in a policy, but he didn't speak to that. Instead, he discussed Stryker's use of "his" computer. "I can only recall one or two times when somebody was waiting to get on it, and he co-operated when I asked him to get off. Nearly always we have another computer somebody can use. Plus you need to understand the library just isn't used very much."

For the first time Judge Morrison spoke. "I agree with Jason. Obviously, we don't have time today to write a new policy. But now I think maybe we *should* meet in one month; this shouldn't wait for two. Jason, since you won't be here then, you can email me your ideas. Let's try to have proposed language ready before the meeting. Henry, I'll get it to you and you can put it on the agenda. And honestly, I think it would be an upgrade if you emailed the agenda and your report to us in advance, so we can read them before we get here."

Daniels nodded as he said, "I'll do that."

The time was 12:23. The president spoke. "Let's see. A lot has happened here in the last few minutes. I think we need a motion to put the pieces together." He took out his tablet again and consulted the calendar.

Brock said, "I move . . ." and efficiently summarized the members' suggestions about a writing a new policy and setting a different date.

"Second?" the president invited.

"Second," said Judge Morrison.

Daniels was rapidly scribbling far more notes than usual, in order to keep track of the actions and later put them in the minutes. Then he was dumbstruck to hear Stryker's voice.

"If you people are going to write some policy as a way of getting rid of me, you won't be allowed to vote on it, Judge Morrison, because, as everyone here needs to understand, you have a conflict of interest—you're hearing my case in your court."

Everyone's eyes turned to her.

"Mr. Stryker," she said with great force, "you are in *so far* over your head. As when you spoke earlier, just because you happen to have an opinion doesn't mean it makes any sense." She paused, as if she was moving to a second bullet point or starting a new paragraph. "Anything between you and me having to do with your case *must* be heard in my courtroom—and only there." Another pause. "And at the moment, assuming I wanted to, I don't have enough time to explain to you what 'conflict of interest' means."

With that the meeting was over. The trustees made their way out of the library. Daniels had previously observed that Judge Morrison was a mentor to the young woman attorney. Now, still sitting at the table, he could hear them laughing together as they left.

The president, hurrying away to his next meeting, called back over his shoulder what he always said at the end: "Thank you, Henry."

Usually the librarian replied to him, "Thank *you*," but this time he felt too drained to say a word. He looked at Stryker, who glared at him for an instant, then rose and stalked out.

Another man had a distinctive way of arriving at the library: planting both legs wide across the threshold, placing his hands on his hips, silently proclaiming "I am here." His camouflage jacket and old cargo pants were remarkably dirty, a description that extended to his hair and even to the lenses of his glasses. If not grubby exactly, there was something pasty even about the texture of the skin of his face. This was Christopher Burke. Daniels had learned he lived alone in a very remote part of the county, a fact that explained the infrequency of Burke's trips to Grant City, perhaps even his hygiene. After entering, he wasn't at all shy about seating himself in the desk chair in front of the library computer, a posture which opened the jacket enough to reveal his ample and hairy belly.

His legal business involved a long-running effort to reclaim some firearms confiscated by the sheriff's department. He communicated updates about this matter to Daniels in a way that seemed to accept the glacial pace of the proceedings. Not that he wasn't serious about the effort; indeed, he maintained permanent outrage over the trampling of his rights. Yet, Daniels thought, Burke at the same time regarded with dry amusement his confrontation with the courts.

Forms

ONE OF THE MOST COMMON TASKS undertaken by patrons of the law library was the filling out of forms. As mundane and bureaucratic as it sounds, the process also represented the workings of a vast system employed throughout California: identical forms in use in every county, making that system—relatively—simplified and efficient. By assisting people with forms, Henry Daniels learned more of the fundamentals of law; both the terminology and the required information on them clarified the legal process.

Because there were hundreds of different forms for the enormous variety of legal matters, Daniels needed to know how to find one that would suit a patron's needs. For this there was a well-organized website containing many (but by no means all) forms, sponsored by a body called the Judicial Council of California, and the librarian had learned to navigate pretty knowledgeably there. Besides being readable on the computer screen, each form was potentially "fillable"; he showed the person how it was possible to fill in needed information on the form by using the keyboard, and then later print it out. Not infrequently, though, because the patron would admit as much or because Daniels could tell, the person wasn't comfortable enough operating a computer to make that "fillability" of any value.

A person wanting to sue someone (maybe a non-human) had to fill out the form titled "Complaint" (hence making the initiator the "plaintiff"). The plaintiff also had to complete a separate form called "Summons" (in the Spanish translation *Aviso*). Its purpose was to inform the opposing party—the defendant—that he or she was being sued. California statutes specified procedures the plaintiff had to follow in order to make sure the defendant learned about the lawsuit.

Once the defendant received the complaint, he or she had a prescribed number of days in which to respond, using a different form titled "Answer." Doing nothing, or waiting too long to do something, automatically resulted in the plaintiff's triumph in court.

Both plaintiffs and defendants had to pay "filing fees" at the of time of submitting forms to the Clerk of the Court. A very small percentage of those fees comprised nearly all the library's stream of revenue. Among the forms were some the parties could use in an effort to obtain a "fee waiver"; if a judge agreed to waive a fee, then the library got no revenue from the filing. Daniels was very much inclined to be sympathetic toward people without the ability to pay, but when he saw those forms in certain people's hands, something less than needy about them made him question their seeking a waiver. And in every case he couldn't help but regret the impact on the library's income if the waiver were granted.

One day a woman related some of the facts of her situation to Henry Daniels. She had received a letter from the office of a doctor in Grant City stating that if she didn't pay the amount it claimed she owed for the doctor's services, then the matter would be turned over to a collection agency, which would sue her and collect the money by court order.

The manner in which she told her story the librarian found quite vague. She seemed to dispute the claim itself: yes, she had seen the doctor, but he didn't perform all the services the letter identified, and she insisted she certainly didn't benefit from his "treatment." Daniels naturally wanted to know more about the type of ailment or condition that had led her to the doctor, but he chose not to ask, and she offered no information that enlightened him. She said she had made a telephone call to the office but hadn't been able to speak with the doctor himself. Instead, the receptionist connected her with someone else in the office who, the woman said, was not at all helpful, in fact was "rude." That person insisted the bill was correct. The library patron repeated her request to talk to the doctor but never received a return call. Apparently, Daniels theorized, she let the matter drift by neither trying again to call the office nor paying any money. In the course of her account, which she interrupted with muttered asides and odd commentary, she also said there was no way she could afford the whole charge.

After listening to her, then asking a few questions in an effort to understand more, Daniels seated the woman in front of some reference books he pulled from the shelves, which he hoped would inform and educate her.

She visited the library again on two occasions; on the first of them she and Daniels didn't have much interaction, but enough to suggest that she was dealing with something altogether different than the doctor bill. Daniels remembered her well. Her appearance was extremely plain, both in clothing and facial features, her body large but not much overweight, her gray hair pinned simply back. Perhaps most distinctive was her manner of speech, which Daniels found wispy and distracted, sometimes even to the point that he wondered if she were speaking to herself. And she seemed depressed, cast down in an air of doubt and defeat.

On her next visit, because he could see she was holding papers bearing the court clerk's official stamp, the librarian could tell the doctor matter had advanced to the point where she would be required to complete forms. Instead of setting her up again with reference materials, he led her to one of the public-access computers.

"I don't know how to use those things," she said in her worried way.

"Well," Daniels replied, "I can bring up the form you need to fill out. We can look at it, and you'll get some idea of what the form is all about. OK?"

She nodded but didn't actually say yes. Everything in her body language said she was relying on him. He sat down, pulled another chair over, and invited her to sit beside him. From there, without much understanding, she observed him go to the Judicial Council website and select the category called "Pleadings."

"If you don't mind, let me see those papers," he said. She handed them to him. He thought he was going to teach her a little about forms, but he discovered immediately that she was confronting a situation quite different from the one he'd expected. Instead of "Summons" and "Complaint" the form she'd received was an "Order to Appear for Examination." Abruptly, visible to no one but keenly felt nonetheless, a wave of humiliation swept across him, accentuating the narrow limits of his knowledge of law.

74

He waited for the wave to subside somewhat before he spoke to her. "Honestly, I-I-I'm not familiar with these forms. I know I need to do some research before I can give you any help."

Again she nodded but without saying anything. He felt his mind divided and racing ahead, in part trying to read her as a person, in part challenged to learn more about her situation, in part remembering the stricture against law librarians practicing law.

His reading of her told him she understood next to nothing about this legal matter. Because of her wispy manner, perhaps as one component of it, he regarded her as a simple person, someone of low intelligence. Even if he'd been right about her needing to fill out an "Answer," her ability to do so was very doubtful. Since now he could see that a totally unfamiliar form was responsible for the pressure on her, and since he himself didn't know how to respond to it, he was certain she didn't either. Still inflamed by a burning in his ears, he felt challenged by his perception of her to learn a great deal more about this area of law. But what would he do with an increase of knowledge? How, given the intellect of the woman, could he share what he learned without, in effect, giving her legal advice?

He studied the several forms she'd handed him, looking for a date that set any sort of deadline, a time by which she would need to take action if she wanted to resist, or at least stall. There seemed to be a way for her to claim an exemption of some kind, but the form said if she wanted to make such a claim she had to do it within so many days of the date of the "Order to Appear for Examination."

He looked at her. Her eyes slipped away from meeting his directly.

"Can you come back tomorrow?" he asked. "That way I'll have some time to study this and then be much more able to help you."

"Yes," she said. "Thank you."

He suggested a time about half an hour after the library would open, and she agreed to return.

"If it's all right with you, I'll keep the papers," he said.

"Yes," she said. "Thank you." Then she stood up and left.

No one else was in the library and he had no other pressing work to do, so Daniels stayed at the computer and proceeded to educate himself. Each Judicial Council form was identified in the upper-right corner of its first page by a simple code, a combination of letters and numbers. So besides being able to read the entire form he held in his hand, he was easily able to determine in what *category* of forms it was included, namely, EJ—Enforcement of Judgment. Knowing that much, he browsed other forms in the EJ category, which gave him a better sense of how the legal system handled debt collection. One form, unhelpfully titled "Abstract of Judgment" (EJ-001), was apparently issued by the court at the point when the "judgment creditor" was authorized to collect the debt.

Daniels also went to search the vast set called *California Forms of Pleading and Practice.* He learned that the debt collector, or collection agency, was the "assignee." The doctor had sold the debt to the assignee, getting it off the doctor's books and thus available as a write-off at tax time. Meanwhile the assignee could

76

concentrate on collecting money from the "judgment debtor," using the legal procedures Daniels was finding out about.

In his reading he came across numerous references to a California law called the Fair Debt Collection Practices Act. Before long he reached up to a high shelf nearby and brought down a volume of the Civil Code, in which he was able to read the complete text of the FDCPA. Interestingly, this law had come into being for the protection of consumers; it listed a great many things that debt collectors were *not* allowed to do. He wondered whether he could— and should—engage the woman in conversation to the level of detail where he'd ask her, for example, "Have you ever gotten any threatening phone calls?"

On other forms in the Enforcement of Judgment category, he found one that contained a long list of allowable exemptions: protected assets beyond the reach of the assignee. He'd heard her say something about not being able to afford to pay the debt but he had no idea regarding the sources of her income. Was she employed? If so, the collector could proceed into the "Garnishment of Wages" category and eventually satisfy the debt that way. But Daniels pondered again the impression he'd had of her as simple—perhaps simpleminded. Was it possible she received some form of disability payment? He knew of a type of Social Security called SSI, intended not exclusively for people over 65 but for people unable to make a living.

If she could pick out one or more exemptions that might apply to her, the librarian thought, she could presumably bring it/them to the attention of the judge. No matter what the validity of her claim, though, the notion of the woman going into court on her own struck Daniels as a losing proposition; if she seemed lost in the law library, how could she possibly fare well there?

The old conflict regarding how much help to give a patron rose again. From past experience he'd come to feel fully at ease sitting at the computer and filling out forms with required information, which he'd obtain by asking the patron for it. It wasn't difficult to satisfy himself that such assistance came nowhere near being "the unauthorized practice of law." At the same time he recognized that sticklers for obedience to the language of the pertinent sections in the Business and Professions Code might argue he was doing just that.

He admitted to himself that what he was doing for the woman was probably going far over the "bright line." As he learned more and more about her legal situation, though, he felt increasingly tempted to cross it.

A few other people who needed a little assistance came into the library. Helping them consumed most of his remaining time. He figured he could continue his research early the next day, but already he'd absorbed so much about debt collection that he found himself excited to be able now to tell her things he didn't know before she'd left.

A few minutes before 9:00 the next morning as usual, he unlocked the door and tended to routine first-thing tasks. His conversation with the woman had pointed toward her arriving around 9:30. When she didn't appear then or for a long time afterward, he tried not to be irritated. Still, the degree of anticipation that had built up since the previous day kept him looking toward the threshold, expecting to see her.

Since no one else came in, he resumed the research, intending to deepen his understanding and prepare specifically for their conversation. There were quite a few forms in the Enforcement of Judgment category, and he scanned their titles again, speculating (with better educated guesses now) as to which ones might fit the woman's case. He couldn't help but consider how and to what extent he'd encourage her to tell more about herself. Clearly, there could be no strategy of seeking an exemption unless she was willing to share personal information about how she lived. When he again studied the form containing the list of allowable exemptions, he decided to print out just the page with that list, intending to hand it to her and ask whether she thought any of them might apply to her. That approach, he hoped, would eliminate any need to interview her at length.

Looming, of course, above and behind all his efforts was the question of how to translate even a promising meeting in the law library into concrete success in court. During the night he'd set aside his fantasies of serving as her advocate and racked his brain to come up with the name of anyone to whom he might conceivably pass along information about her case. At best, as far as he knew, a lawyer would only take it on a contingency basis, meaning that legal representation would cost her nothing unless she escaped the debt; but at that point the lawyer would demand a substantial percentage of what she had "won," which would simply amount to another debt.   And since she didn't stand to win any money anyway, there being thus basically nothing in it for the lawyer, why would anyone bother? Daniels knew full well the matter wasn't one of major social justice, something a public-minded attorney might get involved with *pro bono*. Nevertheless, the case—even despite the oddity of the woman—nagged at him, as if, unlike a lawyer, he didn't get to pick and choose which fight to fight.

At around 10:30 she drifted in. Seeing him at the computer, she approached.

"Did you find out anything?" she asked.

"I did," he answered. "Quite a bit." He hesitated but then went ahead to say, "I thought you'd be here before now."

"Ohh," she responded, her voice falling. "I wasn't sure. And I had some other things I had to do."

He asked her two questions: "Do you drive? Do you live around here?"

"They took my license away. I walk. Sometimes the bus."

He encouraged her to sit beside him. "From my studying I realize that to help you I need to know more about you. OK?"

When she nodded but didn't speak, he recognized the pattern as a habit.

He handed her the printed-out paper and said, "Look this over, will you? What we need to know is whether any of them—they're a list of things people own and ways they get money—whether any of them fits with you."

"But what does that have to do with my debt?"

"You see up here, the title of the page? These are all what are called 'Exemptions,' meaning they're exempt, they're protected, from debt collection"

She began reading the list. "I never heard of some of these things," she said.

"Don't worry. That's all right. Most of them don't have anything to do with most people. But go slow and look for anything you think has to do with you."

Suddenly a man burst into the library. When he saw the woman sitting with Daniels, he immediately rushed over to her. "Jane! Where have you been? I've been looking all over for you!"

Jane squirmed in her chair but didn't answer him.

"Excuse me," Daniels said, "I've been trying to give her some help. Who are you? Why are you talking to her that way?"

"Would you just stay out of this," the man commanded. "You don't know anything about her, and it's none of your business to find out."

Daniels deeply resented the man's tone but tried to remain calm as he responded, "I know at least a little about her. She's come in here several times and explained the legal matter she has to deal with." He was about to repeat something about trying to help her, but the man cut him off.

"Jane! Is that true? You know you're supposed to come to me for—for pretty much everything. So what do you mean by coming in here? Let's be real: you don't know how to read these books."

"I still don't have any idea who you are," Daniels insisted. "So I really don't understand how you can speak to her like that."

"Listen," the man said, and he began to add "I . . ." But he cut himself off and started over. "Where do you fit into the picture here?" he asked Daniels with a sneer. "What's your job?"

"I'm the law librarian. I try to help people who ask for help."

"That sounds very nice," the man said. "Very nice indeed." Daniels heard the sarcasm getting thicker. "I'm sure you're very good at what you do."

"But . . ."

"Yes indeed, there's a 'but.'" He sighed and then spoke more slowly and deliberately, as if having to explain something to a child. "Jane here is not just any 'people who ask for help.' And even if I wanted to, the law does not permit me to explain to you what that means, or who I am, or why she should never even have come to your library."

A part of Daniels, as he questioned the man's words and continued resenting his tone, felt an injustice must be unfolding. But a far larger part of him felt as confused as when he realized he was all wrong about forms. He looked over at Jane. She was looking down at her hands resting heavily in her lap.

"Come on, Jane, we're leaving." This time there was quite a different tone, more gentle, in the man's voice. She stood and followed him out of the room.

Daniels felt empty. There was nothing he could do.

A contemporary of Daniels whom he'd known for years stopped in from time to time. By chance they'd been born and grew up in different parts of the same large Midwestern city but had never known each other there; even so, they found ways to reminisce about it. Robin Barrett had begun his career as a newspaper reporter with a morning daily in that city. Daniels' first work as a teacher was in an East Coast state.

When they met, in Grant City, it was as fellow journalists on The Manzanita Bark, *an "alternative" weekly newspaper. Expressive of its era, it was intended idealistically to cover the whole huge county. The two men admired each other's writing and became friends, with several more interests in common.*

In the law library their conversation was often about sports. For Barrett this meant baseball only; he forthrightly stated his lack of interest in basketball, football, or hockey. Growing up in the Midwest, both of them naturally were fans of the city's American League team. Later, after several years in California paying no attention to baseball whatsoever, Daniels resumed being a fan but switched allegiance to the San Francisco Giants, in the National League. Barrett remained utterly loyal to the original club. Occasionally he would travel to Oakland to see them play the A's.

After the Bark *folded Daniels returned to teaching. Barrett began a long career as an investigator for the county's public defender. No doubt he acquired other skills on that job, but certainly he was using his reportorial skills to great advantage, and to the librarian he appeared to thrive in the world of criminal defendants and their lawyers.*

As a small sideline, Barrett wrote a column published in the Sunday edition of the Grant City Gazette *(definitely not an "alternative" paper). It ran there under a pseudonym, Billy Bob Barnett, and was accompanied each week by a few sentences in italics, with different messages each week but which all suggested that Robin Barrett and Billy Bob Barnett significantly overlapped. The alias was a curmudgeon. Yet, Daniels thought, despite the columns' maintenance of that thorny outlook, a high percentage of them contained large grains of truth.*

He theorized that Barrett's line of work since the Bark *days had darkened his view of humanity. But it was only a theory, and they rarely talked about it. Instead, the investigator was inclined to sustain their friendship by talking about literature. His own preferences included but were by no means limited to Elmore Leonard and Carl Hiaasen; he knew 19th and early-20th-century American lit, naming Ambrose Bierce his favorite author. Barrett was impressed to learn somewhere that Daniels once read all of* À la recherche du temps perdu *(in English). Haltingly, the librarian tried to convey what he had found masterful in Proust.*

Trumpist

EVEN AS AN ORDINARY CITIZEN, in other words
apart from his job at the library, Henry Daniels paid a lot of
attention to matters of law. News about the U.S. Supreme
Court routinely reached him, and he followed decisions by
its nine justices involving health care, gun control,
affirmative action, voting rights, labor unions, environmental regulation, campaign financing, abortion, et al. He
understood that the legal reasoning behind those decisions
was often quite complex, resting on precedents, balancing,
differing standards of judging evidence, and other
distinctions that, he had to admit, were over his head. But
he also figured, if they were over *his* head, then a huge
percentage of the American public, to the extent it was
aware of such cases at all, was surely forming its opinions
on a drastic lack of legal knowledge and critical thinking.

To him it was a given that in mass society there were
broad differences among the population; even while the
paths of jurisprudence trod by the nine were worlds away
from what common people understood, he'd held a general
belief that split decisions by the Supreme Court somehow
reflected those differences. Attempting to understand the
justices' philosophies (labeled simplistically, he thought, as
"liberal" and "conservative"), he'd tended to credit those
women and men with intellectual integrity and moral
reasoning in their position at the apex of the country's
courts.

But lately this confidence in their fair-mindedness was being eroded by what struck him as nakedly political motivation. It was one thing to acknowledge that political thinking dominated the other two branches of the federal government; the officeholders in them, after all, were elected. By definition this meant they'd represent—but also frequently pander to—voters. By contrast, early in his own education Daniels was indoctrinated with the notion that Supreme Court justices, because they were appointed for life, rose above politics. But case after recent case kept challenging that notion, forcing him to conclude that the political party of the President who appointed him was the single most important factor in the justice's reaching a decision. "Originalists" seemed all the more hypocritical to Daniels when, while claiming to adhere to constitutional chapter and verse, they consistently cast votes applauded by Republicans. (Perhaps, he had to acknowledge, the shoe fit also on the other foot, meaning Breyer, Ginsburg, Kagan, and Sotomayor reached results Democrats really liked.)

Some of the attorneys who plied their trade in the Manzanita County Courthouse were relatively plain in wardrobe and manner, but Daniels viewed many of them as extremes of sartorial and behavioral pomp. Suit and tie were extremely rare in the vast rural areas of the county, and quite uncommon in Grant City, the small-town county seat. Yet inside the courthouse those peacocks strutted, haughtily proud of the status society conferred upon them as "officers of the court." At $300+ per hour, all of them, plain and fancy alike, were gatekeepers whose rates enabled access (to "justice") for the affluent and barred it to the hoi polloi. There was unquestionably an old-boy network (including a few high-powered females) visible and audible from the library's front desk. This was particularly true on Friday mornings, prior to the opening of the doors of Courtroom E for that day's calendar of hearings on motions. No matter which side of a case they were about to go in and argue, the barristers greeted one another heartily, in a hallway that amplified their good cheer.

Some when they needed to cross the threshold seemed to treat Daniels in friendly enough fashion, but over time he came to regard it as master-servant friendliness, easily set aside in other settings where fraternizing with the help was inappropriate. One guy in particular, George Lukasik, probably visited the law library more frequently than any other attorney. This was in part because his office was a very short distance from the courthouse, in part because, as a sole practitioner, he relied on the library's free resources rather than maintain expensive subscriptions on his own. Lukasik's occasional outfit of canary-yellow slacks and aqua tie struck Daniels as loud, but much more so it attested to the man's presentation of a super-sized self.

Some of his time in the library was spent examining hardcover volumes, particularly California appellate cases he thought would bolster legal arguments he was constructing. He'd sit with the books for a time, taking notes on the ubiquitous yellow legal pad, then eventually borrow an armload of them (a library privilege reserved exclusively for lawyers). Not infrequently he'd ask Daniels to log on to Westlaw, in order that his legal research could be conducted via that phenomenal electronic tool, after which Daniels often would also do the searching, since

Lukasik, trained in an earlier era, for the most part didn't know how. The attorney's tone in asking for assistance betrayed, Daniels thought, an attitude of entitlement; it was not polite, nor did the conclusion of such a session routinely include a thank-you. The librarian silently noted this behavior but at the same time didn't hesitate to employ his skill. It was work he considered part of his job no matter whom he was helping, and besides, navigating Westlaw's vast search engine was fun.

On days when Lukasik wasn't particularly busy, which seemed fairly numerous, he liked to talk to Daniels, or, more accurately, talk *at* him—he wasn't a good listener. Invariably there was a political slant to these monologues: years earlier, at their very first meeting and before Daniels had even spoken, Lukasik slapped him with the label "liberal," for the lawyer a term of sneering opprobrium. This was uncanny. Was there something about the librarian's physical appearance that instantly earned him the "L-word": his thick glasses? his mustache? In truth, within the broad lexicon of American political discourse the term wasn't incorrect, though by the time Daniels began working in the law library he might himself have chosen "progressive."

The librarian regarded as odd but amusing the way Lukasik always, immediately, and repeatedly used the word "liberal" when he saw Daniels, since even while the attorney was buffeting him with it, there seemed to be a very slight note of mocking himself. He was so quick to blame "these liberals" for everything, including even such a *non sequitur* as a broken traffic light on Main Street, that it seemed (or perhaps Daniels hoped) he had a degree of self-awareness. Once their talks proceeded past that

88

inevitable label, they engaged in relatively civil conversation, though always with Lukasik doing most of the talking. He warmed to a variety of neutral topics, from the weather to books to baseball. He talked a great deal about his passion for traveling solo for several weeks, two or three times a year, to the Olympic Mountains of Washington State, to take photographs of craggy peaks, rushing streams, and lush vegetation in the temperate rain forest there. Upon his return he used the photos as the basis for watercolor paintings. He was proud of an extensive collection of cameras, a couple of which he always packed for those trips and employed to capture images he chose on the Olympic Peninsula. On the trips he also read a lot and did who-knew-what-else. He owned and maintained three vintage cars from the '40s and '50s; his fleet also included a year-old BMW, a Dodge Ram, and the Land Rover he always drove to Washington.

Occasionally he discoursed very knowledgeably on a legal topic, such as the history of the death penalty in California. Or he would candidly go into close detail about a case he was working on; in one he was trying to collect from an insurance company, for bodily injury and property damage suffered by his client. Despite the density of the information and his knowing that Lukasik liked to hear himself talk, Daniels appreciated learning quite a bit about how a lawyer thinks and works, and, because going up against an insurance company was notoriously difficult, the lesson elicited his silent sympathy. Lukasik even shared what struck Daniels as semi-private information about setbacks in his own education and career. The librarian's slight contributions in these talks were apparently adequate for Lukasik to give him credit for being intelligent—"for a liberal." Still, the benighted ignorance of the latter mindset lay permanently in contrast to the infinitely wiser "conservative" Lukasik considered himself.

In the past Daniels had made what he regarded as sincere efforts to understand conservatism. In college he'd studied Thomas Hobbes, Edmund Burke, and other political philosophers. He remembered the brilliance of William F. Buckley and Charles Krauthammer, read newspaper columns by George Will that he sometimes found incisive, and learned enough to become familiar with von Mises, Hayek, the Chicago School, and Milton Friedman. These names and the ideas associated with them, he thought, comprised the intellectual essence of what had come to be known as the right.

From the beginning of their acquaintance and for many years afterward, Daniels and any passerby could see in one window of Lukasik's office a banner with the words "DON'T TREAD ON ME" and the 13-segment colonial snake wriggling across it. This presumably proclaimed Lukasik's conservatism, in aggressive but more or less unassailable terms (unless one wanted to re-argue the case for the American Revolution); Daniels preferred to see it as an artifact of history rather than as fighting words for contemporary times.

Separate from political labels, and in addition to what he'd learned from him, Daniels thought Lukasik deserved two distinct types of credit. For one, from time to time when the lawyer was in the library a certain type of patron had come in seeking legal information and help. The type was known as a "pro per," from a Latin expression that translated, in effect, as "not represented by an attorney." On more than a few occasions the librarian had observed

Lukasik assist such a person, giving the benefit of his expertise and not charging for it. Convinced that most other lawyers wouldn't be at all so generous, Daniels counted it as an admirable trait in Lukasik's character.

The other credit derived from a time when Lukasik arranged for eight or ten of his watercolors to hang for several weeks on the brick walls inside Schindler's, the popular bakery/cafe across the street from the courthouse. Naturally the lawyer talked up the exhibit, including to the librarian, and eventually, though unlike so many courthouse regulars he rarely went to Schindler's, Daniels dropped in to see it. As he studied the paintings first from afar and then much more closely, he was moved by their undeniable beauty—what skill it had taken to make them. He realized that one of the purposes of Lukasik's spending so much time in the Olympics was to enable him to capture the exquisite light there; he must have had to wait many many hours until the illumination was just what he sought. The paintings proved that Lukasik was an artist, a tribute Daniels conceded but uneasily. His knowledge of the history of art had taught him there was no necessary correlation between the work and the character of the artist. The qualities of the attorney he found so annoying in no way reduced the excellence of the watercolorist's creations.

Despite these mitigating factors in the librarian's perception of the lawyer, a crucial turning point—at least from Daniels' point of view—arose during the presidential campaign of 2016: Lukasik removed "DON'T TREAD ON ME" and replaced it with a poster blaring support for "TRUMP / PENCE / MAKE AMERICA GREAT AGAIN." Abruptly, the librarian could no longer rationalize the window display but instead had to confront in it Lukasik's total support for a candidate—and then, incredibly, a president—Daniels utterly despised. This made it a great deal harder for him to maintain cordiality toward the attorney, who continued to frequent the library, taunt him with the L-word, and comfortably engage in their typical one-way conversation.

It was astonishing to the law librarian that Lukasik not only refused to acknowledge the unbridgeable abyss between Donald Trump and traditional conservatism—George Will was a staunch and principled opponent—but unashamedly endorsed everything about him. Trump, widely known not to read, undoubtedly knew little about theories of small government and powers reserved to the states; not only Daniels but, he wanted to believe, millions of others also saw him as a vulgarian with an impoverished vocabulary, a continual liar, a racist and sexist boor.

The makeup of the Supreme Court rose to the forefront of public attention during—no, actually *before*—Trump's being in the White House. In 2016 Antonin Scalia died suddenly, during Barack Obama's presidency, many months prior to the November election. According to the Constitution, Obama had the authority and responsibility to fill a Supreme Court vacancy, and he carried those out by nominating Merritt Garland. But then, violating all precedent, the Republicans, who controlled the Senate, refused even to schedule hearings at which to consider confirming the nominee. McConnell of Kentucky, the majority leader, brazenly declared that the nomination should be made and considered *after* the election, by whomever would succeed Obama—a procedure utterly inconsistent with the Constitution but totally in line with the Republicans' one and only strategy: oppose everything Obama.

Right after being elected Trump named Neil Gorsuch; the Senate quickly did its thing, and Gorsuch became a justice. Later, a year and a half into Trump's reign, Anthony Kennedy announced his retirement. With the Senate still controlled by McConnell and the Republicans, this gave Trump the opportunity to demolish the so-called "swing vote" and create a court majority likely to last for decades.

Around this time Lukasik apparently went on one of his photography retreats, so when Daniels next saw him it had been months since the two had spoken. His entering the library one morning was, predictably, accompanied by a mocking potshot at the librarian.

"How's the liberal today?" he asked. "Still on the wrong side of everything?"

The questions presented the librarian with a challenge he'd easily ignored in the past but which now, with the country in what he considered the most dire condition of his lifetime, he couldn't so calmly dismiss. Still, the reflex neutrality he always tried to maintain as law librarian cautioned him against taking the attorney's bait. "Carrying on," he replied, "though not as usual."

"What's different?" Lukasik continued. "You haven't come around to the right way of thinking, have you? And by that I don't mean 'politically correct.'"

"Not at all. It's just that I've never seen right be so wrong."

As was his habit the attorney laughed, briefly but genuinely, at Daniels' wordplay. "Actually I agree. It *is* a special moment."

"How so?"

"The Supreme Court. Finally—a chance to make the liberals irrelevant."

"You'd really like that, wouldn't you? Then Republicans would control the White House, Congress, *and* the court. So much for checks and balances. How about getting rid of elections too?"

"Now, now, don't get carried away. I think I'm talking to a sore loser."

"Maybe so," Daniels muttered, his neutrality pledge tugging.

At that point Lukasik moved to the rear of the library, and Daniels resumed the rudimentary tasks he'd been doing prior to the attorney's entrance. He couldn't help replaying their exchange in his head; he found no fault in anything he'd said but felt nagged by an unaccustomed desire to argue.

Another patron entered soon thereafter, a "pro per" who'd been issued a speeding ticket by the California Highway Patrol. Hoping to fight it in court, where he was scheduled to appear a short time later, the man wanted to look at statutory language, to see if anything there might give him a way to defend himself. Daniels led the way to the shelves holding all the California codes, including, near the end of their alphabetical order, the three volumes of the Vehicle Code.

"Let me see the ticket, will you?" Daniels asked the man. What he saw was an extremely fuzzy copy of the original ticket, the latter presumably having first been written by the officer and later filed with the court. Perhaps there were more than just the original and the one in his hand. In any case, he wondered, was it possible the CHP was still making *carbon* copies?

Although he personally had the opposite of sympathy for drunks behind the wheel, street racers, and other reckless drivers, his initial tendency as law librarian was to side with anyone who asked for his help. In this situation, he wondered whether the near-illegibility of the writing that supposedly identified which Vehicle Code section had been violated might provide the patron with a defense.

"I can't even read this," he remarked. "Maybe if you go into court and say you can't even figure out what law you broke, it could get you out of it." As he looked more closely, he also couldn't read the name of the officer, and it appeared the lines after "date" and "time" were blank. He said to the man that those were additional reasons why the ticket might not be valid.

The librarian knew that by using the thick master index to all the twenty-nine codes he would almost certainly be able to find the pertinent sections on speeding. But before he even reached for that book or ventured any more thoughts aloud, another voice spoke: "Let me have a look at that." It was Lukasik, sitting so close nearby that he'd easily overheard Daniels. The librarian handed the paper to the lawyer, who skimmed it rapidly before handing it back to the man. "What courtroom are you in?" he asked.

"G. At eleven o'clock."

"Hmm—Judge Ford. He'll know what section it is even if you can't read it. And he always believes cops, too. I'd say your best chance is if the CHP guy doesn't show up. They're really busy, have to cover a huge territory, and I've seen lots of times they don't make it to the hearing. You don't have a lawyer, am I right?"

"Right."

"So I'd say, when your name is called, if the cop isn't there, right away ask the judge to dismiss the case. I can't tell you what he'll do. He might continue it to another day. He might make you wait somehow, to buy time for the CHP guy to walk in. He might give you a lecture but end up saying 'Case dismissed.'"

Looking a little stunned, the man said, "I don't know how to thank . . ."

"Don't get caught next time," Lukasik chimed in, laughing, as the man left.

Daniels, despite still fiercely wanting to challenge Lukasik on the national crisis, had to admire his again-demonstrated willingness to dispense free advice. As he stood adjacent to the lawyer's spread of yellow pads and lawbooks, what emerged from his mouth wove those two incongruous strands of his thought: "Was that conservatism in action?"

"Spoken like a liberal," Lukasik answered. "You're mixing apples and oranges. Though I guess I'd say liberals are kind of fruity."

"*Now* what do you mean? About the mixing. I'll ignore the 'fruity.'"

"I practice law to make a living. That's why you've noticed my car parked downtown on weekends sometimes. And, believe it or not, I enjoy helping people cut through the system. None of that is about ideology."

"Wait a minute. You can't just claim you're Joe Everyman, Esquire. You go out of your way to broadcast your politics. Why do you slap me around as a 'liberal'?" And why do you have that damn Trump sign in your window?"

"Ah, right, now we're getting down to what really bugs you."

"Damn right, pardon my French again. I despise him. He's absolutely the worst president I've ever seen—and I'm older than maybe you think. Yeah, of course I believe people are going to have different opinions about things, and of course they're free to have them. But this really is different. I simply can't understand how people can listen to him tell lies and act like a pig and still support him."

"There now. Good. Take a deep breath. Do you feel better yet?"

"Quit it! You won't take me seriously!" Daniels resented Lukasik's condescension, but this response to it sounded in his own ears like a kid whining.

"Oh please," the lawyer continued. "Who *are* you, anyway? A lousy law librarian in Podunk County, California. Yeah, I guess I've granted that you're equipped with a brain, but doing that was just a courtesy. Besides being totally wrong, your opinions simply don't count."

Daniels was aware he had started this and that he didn't at all know how to finish it. Lukasik's insults stung, which pushed him further into arguing. At the same time, he envisioned someone walking into the library and finding the two of them embroiled.

"Thanks for that," he said, "thanks a lot. It's really nice to be appreciated. Also you're welcome for being your peon on Westlaw."

"C'mon—it's your job."

"This is going nowhere." Daniels took a breath— maybe the one Lukasik suggested. "You still haven't explained to me why you're for Trump. Are you really not seeing the same things I am?"

Lukasik appeared to think about the question before he spoke. "All right," he began slowly, "I'll put it in terms maybe you can understand. And I don't mean you're not smart. I say it that way because people like you are so totally convinced you're 'correct' about everything that it's impossible for you to see things any other way. OK, and don't pass around that you heard this from me, but yes, Trump as one person is pretty much the way you describe him. But that's beside the point. I support him because he's the ANTI-LIBERAL! He represents the best chance in decades to put 'you people' in your place."

Alarms went off in Daniels. "What place is that? Concentration camps?"

"There! My point exactly. You make the standard liberal leap. Who said anything about 'concentration camps'? Not me."

The librarian felt the dead weight of the fact this was an argument he could never win. But he wasn't entirely ready to give up. "So the Supreme Court is going to become conservative hog heaven." His words could have been a question but they came out a statement.

"I know I can't convert you," Lukasik responded, "but at least your vision is improving."

"Hey, I'm not the only one who can see clearly. They couldn't impeach and convict Nixon or even Andrew Johnson. But that doesn't mean it can't happen now. Then where will you and the anti-liberals be? You'll have to put 'DON'T TREAD ON ME' back in your window."

It so happened a woman entered the library at that moment.

Daniels called gently to her across the room. "Can I help you?"

"Yes. I need to make four copies of each page."

"I'll be glad to help you with that."

As he walked toward the copy machine to meet her, Daniels felt relieved to be out of the go-nowhere confrontation.

But then he heard a parting shot from Lukasik aimed at his back. "I know the code about what a law librarian isn't supposed to do. No question you were giving advice to the guy with the speeding ticket." Intended to get under his skin, the comment did its job as Daniels went through the familiar motions of making copies, taking money from the woman, and making change. After she left he sat again at the front desk, squirming beneath the implications of what he couldn't help but interpret as Lukasik's threat.

Lukasik remained at the table in the rear for another half an hour, then brought his briefcase and a stack of books to the desk. Silently, he took his own pen from his shirt pocket and wrote all the required information on the borrowing register. Daniels watched him, also silently, reflecting on how obedient the lawyer was in recording, besides the titles of the books, Lukasik's entirely familiar name and phone number. When he was finished, the attorney strolled comfortably to the threshold, then turned back to say, "Nice talking with you today, Henry. And don't worry about me costing you your job—I'd miss you too much if you weren't here."

For many years before she moved away from Manzanita County, a woman paralegal used the library fairly often. Daniels knew she worked for a personal-injury attorney whose offices were across Main Street from the courthouse; it was rare to see him in the library but every December he graciously sent it a holiday card. The librarian figured the woman had substantial responsibilities for some of his cases; she seemed highly intelligent and very experienced, the sort of assistant on whom an attorney would rely. As with others, though, he never knew what she was researching.

Nearly always she would stop at the front desk, on her way in or out, to make brief conversation with Daniels. Besides that intelligence, as well as her dry sense of humor, slender figure, and the warmth of her smile, he was struck by the extreme softness of her voice—barely above a whisper. He didn't at all mind leaning forward, listening very carefully, to follow what she was saying.

**   **   **

Infrequently a guy entered and talked to Daniels as if they knew each other well, which wasn't true. He appeared to be dressed for a court appearance but, in Daniels' opinion, he looked like a man who otherwise never wore white business shirt (frayed), suit jacket (rumpled), and dark tie. His reason for coming to the library was to make copies of a few papers connected to his case, but he took time to make conversation as if the copying were incidental. Daniels barely spoke and didn't remember the chat as anything other than very small talk; in fact, after a number of repetitions of the entire pattern, he came to the conclusion that the guy was a small-time con artist. For it was the habit of this "patron" not to pay for the copies, instead to cover their minimal cost by scribbling illegible IOUs. The increasing sum of the debt never reaching even two dollars, Daniels found himself so intrigued by the transparency of the grifter that he never insisted on payment.

Investiture

DURING AN EARLY PHASE of his life in Manzanita
County, dropping out of teaching to chase a youthful dream
of writing, Daniels worked at home on what he hoped
would become a novel. At the time he was married, to
another teacher, and she continued at her job, which
supported them both.

Two years later, though, the marriage having slunk to a
bleak end, in order to escape the claustrophobia of Apple
Valley he moved away, first to Johnsville, then to
Comstock, eventually to Grant City. A period of licking
his wounds continued there but finally ended when he was
drawn into the small world of local journalism.

There existed in those days an "alternative" weekly
newspaper called *The Manzanita Bark*, whose offices
occupied the front half of the second floor of an old,
yellow-painted brick building on Main Street. (The
building belonged to, and the back half of its second floor
was used by, the International Order of Odd Fellows.)
Hired to join its staff, Daniels let go of the novelist fantasy
and began writing about the week-in/week-out reality of
the county and city where he lived.

The newspaper was just a few steps from the Manzanita
County Courthouse, which at that time, besides the courts,
housed most of the county departments. Thus, many years
before he ever set foot in the law library, the courthouse
was a very familiar setting where he came to know names
and faces that were prominent in those days. The cub

reporter's first "beat" was the Board of Supervisors, which met in a room that, years later, was converted into Courtroom C. Daniels watched, listened, and took notes on the proceedings of the BoS, which he transformed into a weekly column in the *Bark* titled "Supes Notes." Inevitably, along the way he absorbed a great deal of knowledge about the history of the county. He also copy-edited, proofread, wrote other news, feature stories, play reviews, once even reported on a murder trial.

Daniels recalled his work on the *Manzanita Bark* as a dream job, the best he ever had. (It folded after only a half-dozen years in operation.) Imagine: paid to write! Besides that, being on its staff meant being a member of a family: photographers, editors, other writers, cartoonists, people in layout and pasteup, ad sales, all working hard together every week to put out a lively product.

While for the most part it was others who covered the courts, because the courthouse scene was as small as it was Daniels came to know the judges, by sight anyway. One of the most distinctive—and, others told him, most admired—among them at that time was Judge Malachi O'Hara. He was a man of wiry build, not much above five-and-a-half feet tall, with steel-gray hair strictly parted high and brushed back along both sides of his large head. On a couple of occasions while the Board of Supervisors was in recess, Daniels took a seat in the back of a courtroom where Judge O'Hara was presiding, primarily to gain a fuller sense of the man. One of the most notable things about him, Daniels could hear, was the charming lilt of his voice, an Irish tenor even without singing. But beyond this was an air of exceptional intelligence and dignified calm, neither of them tainted by arrogance. A few times in courthouse hallways the reporter spotted the judge, not in black robe but in white shirt and dark tie, emanating that same air. Judge O'Hara's encounters with others on those occasions, without respect to their station in the legal world, were, as far as Daniels could tell, honest and direct, without affectation, and they left the reporter believing that the judge deserved his reputation.

It wasn't until decades afterward, when he'd gone to work in the law library, that Daniels had his own direct encounters with Judge O'Hara. A few times the judge, by then quite an old man, came into the library looking for a particular volume and asked Daniels to point him in the right direction. Once it was for *Acts and Proceedings of the Legislature of California* from 1850—the year of statehood. After he found what he was looking for in the very old book, he showed it to the librarian; it recorded the establishment of Manzanita as one of the original California counties, including a detailed survey defining its boundaries. The judge didn't specifically say why he was looking for the material but remained long enough to read a little aloud to Daniels, as if he were sharing it. (No one else was in the library.) Even without singing he had, as in Daniels' recollection, that special lilt in his voice. Daniels never forgot the feeling of Judge O'Hara's close presence.

Submerged nearly altogether beneath the law librarian's thoughts about the work he did were others, about roads never taken long before he'd moved to Manzanita County. In the presence of so many lawyers, how could he not wonder about the course of his life had he become one of them? Classmates from high school and college, several whom he still knew well, had gone on to enter that profession. *He* could have chosen to go to law school, he was certain *he* would have passed the bar exam, leading him to an utterly different life.

While as an English teacher he did continue to be a sort of "actor" in the classroom, the role of the law librarian cast him in a chronically passive role. Despite wanting to make some difference in the world, he was obliged not to be an activist there, since by definition he would be advocating—exactly what a law librarian wasn't supposed to do. To a degree this reinforced his commitment to dealing with all sorts of people neutrally, but to a greater extent it magnified a tendency he'd long noticed in himself: observing the world as it passed him by.

It was in the light of such thinking that he observed those lawyers in the courthouse. In so many ways "the system" was built upon and around them: every one was an "officer of the court" who exercised significant power within the workings of that system. Daniels wasn't at all convinced the United States truly functioned under "the rule of law," but there was no question it existed under the rule of lawyers. He acknowledged that his attitude toward the breed was cynical; he did make exceptions, such as for *pro bono* lawyers on The Innocence Project, who advocated on behalf of prisoners treated terribly unjustly.

Indeed, p*ro bono* work and, yes, the very power of every attorney—these retained a sway over Henry Daniels. Despite the workaday business continuously transacted at the Manzanita County Courthouse, the law, in his cynical eyes, did have a certain majesty. And the investiture of a judge was an occasion when, for a few extended moments, that majesty was in the air.

105

"Investiture" was a term with which Daniels made several tentative associations. In the library he consulted Black's Legal Dictionary, where he read it was an oath of office administered by another judge; by reciting it, the new judge promised "to uphold and defend the Constitution, against enemies foreign and domestic." Of course those words echoed exactly the ones spoken at a presidential inauguration. But in this instance was a second meaning: the donning of the judge's long black robe—related to the clothing we call a "vest" perhaps? The robe was a transformative costume, turning an everyday person into a figure of authority and, in the best of cases, majesty. A third association, unlikely to be in the dictionary but it occurred to Daniels anyway, was that the legal profession and the larger community were "investing" their trust in this person, their confidence and expectation that he or she would perform a judge's duties with wisdom, fairness, justice.

The ceremony itself was an opportunity for members of the local bar to celebrate themselves as upholders of a very long tradition. If only by a pressure in the atmosphere of their own presence, these occasions were authentic and high-minded, reinforcing the belief that the law was an honorable profession. There was theater to it also, an audience of friends, colleagues, and well-wishers in front of two rows of current (and a few retired) judges, each in the black robe of the office.

Henry Daniels was present at more than one investiture, but one stood out in his memory. This was because several streams of his personal history in Manzanita County had carried him to that place and time, each contributing to the respect he had for the man of the hour. Though he felt he'd never known the new judge extremely well, the variety of their contacts over many years amounted nearly to a friendship, and throughout that time his admiration for Jordan Reynolds had steadily grown.

The earliest chapters of their paths' crossing coincided with the future judge's moving to Manzanita County, along with a dozen of his fellow graduates of the University of California, Santa Cruz. The unique physical and academic environment of their *alma mater*, perched gloriously on slopes above the Pacific Ocean, had inspired those classmates to move to a rural part of the state for the next phase of their lives. There they proceeded to establish a small school miles outside Grant City and to live there communally, in a mountainous setting where nature was embedded in the curriculum. Because the population of "newcomers" to the county was quite small then, Daniels and his wife (two more teachers) came to know the pioneers from UC Santa Cruz and visited their remarkable school on several occasions.

While *The Manzanita Bark* lasted, Jordan Reynolds contributed a column to it. Before that time he'd gone back to the Bay Area for law school, married a classmate from there, and for many years been in practice in Grant City, specializing in criminal defense. Unlike Daniels not on the staff of *The Bark*, even so he was a member of the paper's "family." Being active as a liberal Democrat supplied him with plenty of material for his column, but he also wrote perceptively and well about life in Manzanita County.

Later, when Daniels tried out the occupation of paralegal, some of the assignments he got came from lawyer-acquaintances, including Jordan Reynolds, who once hired him to investigate a matter of criminal law. Daniels traveled to Fort Pierce to interview the owner and some employees of an auto repair shop; Reynolds was representing a former employee charged with breaking in and stealing several thousand dollars' worth of tools. The paralegal wrote up the results of the interviews, then came to Reynolds' office to discuss them. Their interaction was professional, the tone businesslike, but with the meeting over there was also time for talk about sports, politics, and mutual friends.

Finally, when Daniels became director of the law library, Jordan Reynolds was serving as a member of the Board of Trustees, and the two routinely sat next to each other at Board meetings. The librarian thought the other trustees barely noticed when Reynolds occasionally whispered something ironic just to him.

In California, if for whatever reason a seat on the Superior Court bench becomes vacant in any county, the governor appoints someone to fill it until the next regularly scheduled election. It so happened that a relatively young Manzanita County judge was diagnosed with a cancer that ended his life just two months after it was discovered. This then added to a long list of appointments (of many kinds) the governor needed to make, and in that moment there was additional pressure because he was approaching the end of his second and last allowable term. Given the enormous responsibility of being governor of so vast a state, it was impossible for him to know the judicial who's-who in every one of its fifty-eight counties, and while the media referred to one of his assistants as a "vacancies secretary," even that person was unlikely to know the legal

108

landscape of Manzanita. So the primary engine generating this gubernatorial power was political; any prospects whose ambition drove them to apply for local appointments were most likely to be chosen, assuming background and qualifications were equally excellent, if they were active in the governor's political party.

Wheels ground very slowly in Sacramento. At last, just days before the end of the governor's term, word came that Jordan Reynolds was being appointed to fill the vacancy. He began presiding as soon as official notification was received, but plans were undertaken at the same time for his investiture.

Henry Daniels was gratified to receive an envelope in the library's mail, addressed to him and containing a handsome invitation to the ceremony. It was called for 5:30 on Friday afternoon, January 9. Actually, the setting wouldn't be inside the courthouse but two blocks away, in the century-old home of the women's association called the Sorority of Thursday Night. This building stood on the corner of Church and Sutter streets, where the roots of a massive sequoia both lifted the sidewalk and pressed inexorably against the historic structure's foundation.

Decades earlier this civic group had had far more members than at present, but with a recent infusion of middle-aged females, it was enjoying rejuvenation. Though the women had long ago completed purchase of the building, it needed steady cash flow to cover property taxes, utilities, and the continual need for repainting and repair. For this reason the association not only held its monthly meetings there but also rented the space for gatherings of various kinds, from wedding receptions and anniversary parties to musical and theatrical performances and, of late, *quinceañeras*. Behind a spacious veranda, the high-ceilinged interior consisted primarily of two large rooms, these separated by a wall that could be partially pulled back, in turn creating an open flow between the two. Beyond one room was a kitchen, at the head of the other a small stage.

It so happened that January 9 was a school holiday, which meant Daniels didn't have to race as usual to meet the first of his three classes in the afternoon. Instead, at the end of his morning stint at the law library, he walked slowly home, made lunch, then lay down to read—Edith Wharton's *The House of Mirth*—and before long fell asleep. When he awoke from this pleasant siesta, it was into a house with no electricity. At first he thought the cause might be merely a burned-out lamp bulb beside the couch where he'd reclined. But he soon discovered there was no power anywhere in the house. Early January meant the day would be short, with 5:30 already dark. Even with the power out completely, he knew it would remain light long enough for him to read unaided awhile. Eventually the darkness was nearly total, and then he waited, doing nothing but think.

He'd been looking ahead with pleasure to the investiture, but in his weave of thoughts there were also strands of anxiety. Much of it, he was aware, had to do with his feeling ill-at-ease in the company of lawyers; even with the friendliest of them, it was a sense of not belonging, as if each was in a higher social class. Now, rather than continuing to believe that his long-held observations and judgments of them were objective, he began to admit that, as a manifestation of this class difference, he himself was biased.

The power outage added to his feeling uptight. From the little battery-powered clock beside his bed he knew what time it was. What he didn't know was how far the outage extended across Grant City. Past experience with occasional blackouts had taught him they could be quite localized, with power on just a block or two away; he wondered how the organizers would handle the emergency if in fact there was no power at the women's club building. Those past outages hadn't been uncommon, and most ended rapidly. But this one didn't. As the time drew nearer to 5:30 Daniels thought not only about going downtown soon—a simple enough walk, even in darkness—but also about the strange possibility that the event wouldn't happen at all.

The need to select clothes for the occasion spurred the last waves of his anxiety. In the courthouse he typically wore what he wore as a teacher, dressed (he thought) appropriately for the library job in button-down shirt and sweater but never a jacket or tie. Certain that the lawyers would be more or less dressed up, should he change that look? No matter what he chose, there was slapstick humor in the scene the outage created: cleaning up and dressing in the dark. In the end, what he wore wasn't much dressier than his everyday look, plus a higher-quality overcoat, which he expected to hang in the cloakroom anyway.

Though the streets down which he walked from his house sat quietly in darkness, from two blocks away the clubhouse looked brilliantly alive, both a beacon of light and a hive of activity. When he entered the Thursday Night Club (as it had come to be known) he found the room containing the stage nearly full, with people seated on many rows of folding chairs; the wall of doors was open

111

and pulled back, enabling standees in the adjoining room a good view of the proceedings. In all, Daniels estimated, there was a crowd of two hundred plus, far more than any room in the courthouse could have accommodated.

On the small stage, elbow to elbow all in black robe, were two rowz of six judges each, the judiciary of Manzanita County present to welcome their new colleague. Three others were seated at a table on the floor a few feet in front of the stage, also facing the audience. One, James Davidson, the current presiding judge and consequently the appropriate man to do so, began the proceedings by rising, stepping forward to a lectern, and announcing to everyone what they all knew full well: "We're gathered here this evening . . . ", and at his naming "Jordan Reynolds" there erupted a tremendous burst of cheering from both rooms, a standing ovation loud with triumph, pride, and enthusiasm, which Daniels himself felt quietly part of and amazed by, to the unexpected point of tears.

There were to be several speakers on a short program before the key moment. Judge Davidson called forth Christopher Holbrook, president of the Manzanita County Bar Association. He in turn gracefully presented a bouquet to Anna, the new judge's wife. The couple's two sons were introduced. Then came a succession of speakers, three attorneys saluting Reynolds and bidding him farewell as he departed their ranks.

First came Edward Levinson, who offered a variety of glimpses of Reynolds over the course of four decades: All-State (Iowa) high school scholar-athlete in three sports; the years at and after UC Santa Cruz; the formation of a law partnership between the two men; Reynolds' love of gardening—and politics. Next was Alfred Morgenstern,

112

whose shoulder-length white hair and elaborately tooled cowboy boots marked his flamboyance, as did his booming laugh (which, from the library, Daniels had long ago learned to pick out in the courthouse stairwell). On this occasion, much less wisecracking than usual, indeed with great conviction, he praised his fellow practitioner of criminal defense. A native son of Manzanita County, Morgenstern belonged to a family prominent in its legal world for several generations. He quoted himself telling his son Derek when the latter was starting out, also in criminal defense, "You can't do any better than to model yourself on Jordan Reynolds." Last was Helen Merrifield, a brilliant woman every ounce the equal of the preceding males, and the superior of all but a few men in adventurous living: she ran marathons and climbed 10,000+-foot mountains. She lived and practiced in the county but also often traveled long distance to represent clients in federal court, particularly to defend their civil rights. Bestowing on Reynolds a set of books whose titles highlighted the differences between lawyers and judges, with great wit she respectfully mocked the judiciary seated above and behind her, garnering huge laughs from the audience.

After these tributes came the formal swearing-in. Judge Davidson, the evening's emcee, introduced the retired Judge Malachi O'Hara for the performance of this honor and announced that Jordan Reynolds had requested that Judge O'Hara play this role. Judge O'Hara and Jordan Reynolds stepped forward to the lectern, where the retired judge proceeded to administer the oath of office and hold out the black robe for the new judge to don. Since Reynolds was quite a bit taller than the older man, he stooped to make the job easier. Then Judge O'Hara pronounced the investiture official and the two heartily shook hands. This triggered another burst of acclaim from the crowd, the sustained cheer surpassing even their earlier one: everyone in the building knew the moment was special.

When this small-town roar subsided, the new judge gave a short speech, seeming very poised and comfortable, both thoughtful and in his low-key way excited, as he thanked a variety of others and pledged himself to the ideal of fairness. At the moment he thanked his wife as "my inspiration," his voice choked with emotion. "I've got this habit of tearing up," he admitted, "which may be okay at a wedding but probably not at the sentencing phase." There were some more funny lines about his new job, evidently prepared in advance but delivered expertly nonetheless; for example, recalling earlier days when he'd been a regular at a long-gone bar frequented by lawyers, he rejected the phrase "sober as a judge" as probably not befitting himself. As to the subtle matter of what he should be called now, he invited people to keep knowing him as "Jordan" in the hallways but insisted that in the courtroom "Your Honor" would be the rule. He paid special tribute to Judge O'Hara, praising the treatment he'd always received in the latter's court, admiring his detailed knowledge of Manzanita County and California law, vowing to strive to emulate his common sense and good judgment.

Another standing ovation greeted the conclusion of this speech, and then most of the crowd moved, mainly into the adjoining room, where there was an open bar and tables full of *hors d'oeuvres*. The strength of Daniels' emotion impelled him to congratulate the new judge, whom he saw at one point not totally mobbed by well-wishers. But his unease prevented him from talking much; he quickly shook Reynolds' extended hand, muttered something more or less appropriate, then moved past.

The reception room was a scene of the legal world drinking: attorneys in loud collegial conversation punctuated by aggressive laughter, definitely not where the law librarian felt comfortable. On its margins he found other people he knew and talked in platitudes with two or three. But before long his desire to leave was far stronger than his reason to stay. He escaped into the darkness.

Usually Daniels was an Albertson's shopper because the supermarket was closest to his home, but from time to time he went to Oliver's, for variety. He was there on a late Sunday morning two days after the investiture. Besides cruising the aisles for the items on his mental list, as always he found it interesting to look at the people, and on this occasion he recognized among the shoppers, in apparel solemn enough to make him appear overdressed, Judge Malachi O'Hara. Daniels was especially struck by this because, on the previous day, the *Grant City Gazette* had published an obituary pertaining to Mary Margaret O'Hara, "who died peacefully at home, surrounded by family and friends, on January 6."

Born in Tacoma, Washington, she met her future husband in San Francisco, where they were married at the Presidio in 1958. The account of her life was of course informative about her husband's as well, since the moves the couple made beyond the Bay Area followed the advance of his career; they lived in Sacramento for five years when he worked for the state Attorney General. Then they moved back to Manzanita County, where he had grown up and where his family had lived for four generations. He engaged in the private practice of law, eventually becoming a judge of the Superior Court. They had three daughters, two sons, numerous grandchildren and great-grandchildren. In her own right Mary Margaret O'Hara had been prominent in Grant City for decades; there was a listing in the obituary of some of her memberships and affiliations, from the Republican Women and the Women's Golf Association to the Garden Club and the Manzanita County Historical Society.

Having lived in Manzanita County as long as he had (nowhere near as long as pioneer families and other old-timers), Daniels always read such notices with keen interest, recognizing names and learning connections among local people—as well as wondering what his own obit would one day say.

The librarian and the retired judge happened to check out around the same time and stood in adjacent lines.

"Do you remember me, Judge O'Hara?" the woman in front of Daniels asked him. "I used to work in the courthouse."

"The face is familiar," he said candidly. They chatted briefly as Daniels, still waiting for his turn to unload groceries, watched and eavesdropped. There was a hearing aid behind one of the older man's ears but Daniels, as at the investiture, was impressed by his vigorous demeanor and the undimmed sparkle of his voice.

It so happened that Judge O'Hara's car was parked next to the librarian's in front of Oliver's, and the two returned almost simultaneously. The first car was a white midsize

116

Chevrolet sedan of a very recent year; Daniels drove a venerable blue Civic hatchback displaying signs of its age. Since without the judge's knowing it the librarian had already been paying so much attention to him, he wanted to initiate even minimal conversation. But Daniels hesitated as the judge transferred two bags from a shopping cart into the passenger seat of his car, then drove away. Daniels likewise loaded his one bag but then sat in the driver's seat of the Honda, reflecting. Obviously, there was an enormous amount he didn't know about Judge O'Hara's life. But, if the newspaper was to be believed, it had to be the case that on the day of the investiture the judge had very very recently lost his wife. And was it possible, Daniels wondered, that at Oliver's he had just come from a funeral mass? The conjunction of these happenings mystified him, but at the same time they cast the old judge in even more extraordinary light.

A few times, a woman wearing a knit hat with earflaps and pushing a stroller crossed the threshold. There was never a toddler in the stroller. Maybe once there was a very small dog? As Daniels recalled it, for the woman the stroller was the equivalent of a backpack, her way to carry miscellaneous belongings, yet he'd come to believe she wasn't homeless. The amount of baggage wasn't very great, seemingly easy enough to push, but there was a heavy-leggedness in her walk. She wore thick glasses and had a distracted air. In short, according to Daniels' diagnosis (and though he wasn't happy using an old pejorative): she was loony. The first time she came in, both to the best of his recollection and consistent with his welcoming philosophy, he observed but didn't judge her. On a later occasion, though, when she stood near the front desk and spoke (not necessarily to him), he couldn't avoid the impression that a sort of breeze was blowing among her brain cells. He wondered how she had managed to get the stroller through security at the courthouse entrance. Eventually, while stopping well short of ordering her not to come back, he said something that conveyed the same message, and she never returned. Nonetheless, from his car he continued to see her pushing the stroller, a familiar sight on the sidewalks of Grant City.

This Land Is My Land

DURING HIS DETOUR as a freelance paralegal, Henry
Daniels did one job for Frederick Simonson, a lawyer he'd
known for many years. Simonson's clients were a married
couple whose legal matter was relatively complex, and he
hired Daniels to handle a few of the less difficult pieces.
The legal topic was adverse possession, a concept about
which the paralegal knew next to nothing, but he became
increasingly informed as he went along. The term itself,
"adverse possession," had a sort of guilty ring. As he
learned how the laws of California under certain
circumstances allowed it, though, the guilt went mostly
away.

Given that the entire American legal system was built
on a foundation of private property, to Daniels it came to
seem inevitable that there would be a legal way for one
party to take over the property of another: adverse
possession. Sections of the Civil Code and the Code of
Civil Procedure stated specific criteria for accomplishing
this. For one thing (and this might already have been
completed by the legal owner), the land had to be enclosed,
typically by a fence. In the statutory language of two other
criteria, the "guilty" ring could definitely be heard, for the
action of the would-be adverse possessor had to be both
"hostile" and "notorious." Daniels eventually realized
these terms weren't moral judgments but rather part of the
law's unfamiliar lexicon. In their arcane manner, courts
had defined "hostile" as meaning that the adverse

possessor's intention was clear, and "notorious" that it wasn't a secret. Another criterion had to do with payment of property taxes; if the legal owner failed to pay for five consecutive years—and the adverse possessor paid them instead—this was the strongest reason why title could be recorded in favor of the latter.

Daniels was briefly introduced to Simonson's clients but didn't sit in on their meetings with the attorney, so he had little basis for understanding the overall case or evaluating their motives. The work he was assigned to do focused on obtaining and analyzing records of property tax payments. He discovered that the payment history wasn't ideally straightforward, since the owner as well as the couple had been inconsistent in paying, plus there appeared to be some gaps in the record when the tax hadn't been paid by anyone. The paralegal pointed out these shortcomings to the lawyer. Eventually, despite an easily observable fence and what Simonson advised them was sufficiently strong evidence of "hostility" and "notoriety," the couple conceded the weakness of the tax element and abandoned their effort.

Years later, Daniels having moved (he didn't fully regard it as "risen") to the directorship of the law library, this experience came in handy. He'd long since had to acknowledge that there were scores of legal topics (unlike adverse possession) he knew next to nothing about. Even so, during his years as library assistant he'd often led patrons to reference works where they could study topics on their own, or sometimes he stayed to help them make sense of the material, in the course of doing which he educated himself.

Despite the fact that Mickey Wright lived two-and-a-half hours from Grant City by truck (maybe only ninety-five miles as the crow flies, but the mountain roads in between switched back on themselves interminably), he was still a resident of Manzanita County and from time to time visited the county seat. He'd spend his day there running errands, and occasionally these included visits to the courthouse, where he chatted, seemingly in no hurry, with Daniels. The librarian enjoyed these exchanges, though in a way they confused him, as Wright tended to greet him more warmly and thank him more respectfully than Daniels thought warranted.

Most striking about the man's appearance was his thick head of long, wiry, gray-black hair, which descended into both a very thick beard and a braided ponytail. Not just his plaid shirt, old jeans, and well-worn boots, but also something in the way he carried himself identified him as a Back-to-the-Lander, a fairly recent generation of immigrants to the county. They had repopulated lands pretty much played out by the overcutting of timber and the unsustainable economics of ranching. Wright had a distinctive confidence, an air of strong belief that he was right. Another air Daniels noted about him was an earthy but not unpleasant smell.

His patronage of the library over the years had been for a variety of purposes, most of which he mentioned only briefly to Daniels because he knew enough to be able to pursue them on his own. On his most recent trip, though, he asked for help on a matter about which he admitted he was ignorant. After greeting Daniels in that extra-friendly tone, he posed the question "Know anything about adverse possession?" Years ago, he went on, someone at a potluck used the term and in that setting Wright learned a layman's definition of it: "squatter's rights." Now, however, in connection with a very private idea he said he was contemplating, he knew he needed to learn much much more about what the law actually said.

"I know a little," the librarian replied, pleased to recall his experience working for Simonson. "For sure nowhere near enough to be an expert, but I can show you where to read about it. If you like, tell me about the situation. That'll help me understand better how I can help."

Wright hesitated a few moments before he quietly spoke. "I *would* be willing to tell you about the 'situation,' but the fact is, nobody else even knows about it." He let that information sink in, then added in a whisper, "So I don't want to just stand right here."

No one else was in the library. Intrigued by Wright's confidential offer, Daniels led him to a table adjacent to shelves of reference works on real estate. They sat and Wright began to speak.

"This is kind of complicated—no way to begin, I guess, but to begin. I must have told you I live way out past Comstock, by myself on forty acres. Been there for thirty-four years, and I've built it up into a lot more than was there when I bought it. Well, there's a piece of land right next to me, which I'm pretty sure is 17 acres, and the way to get there is by using the same road I use. There's a cabin on it and a shed, and a kind of funky fence around it, but I never see anybody there. You see where I'm going with this?"

"I think so, but keep going."

"I mentioned the road because if anybody was coming to that parcel, I'd almost certainly know about it. And from what I know about adverse possession, which, I'll tell you, is damn little, the owner has to 'possess' it, at least part of the time, or he's leaving himself—could be a woman, I suppose—open to someone else taking it over. That's what I think is the 'situation' on that parcel, and I've been wondering what I could possibly do to . . ." (he hesitated before finishing) "take it over myself."

At this moment Daniels couldn't be sure about the overall look on his own face, other than to figure it expressed some mix of gratitude for being let in on the secret, admiration for the boldness of the idea, and awareness of the complexities Wright didn't know he was getting into. Behind this expression was the silent question Daniels always asked himself, about how to respond and proceed.

"I brought you back here for privacy, but also because I expected we'd be looking into these," the librarian said before long, motioning to a set of twelve thick black binders titled *California Real Estate*, (which he knew lawyers all referred to by its editors' names: Miller and Starr). "I know there's a whole chapter on adverse possession somewhere in there, which you're gonna need to study if you're serious about your idea." Then quickly he added, "I'm not doubting you're serious. It's just that what you say you want to do is . . . a big deal."

"You think it's worth a shot?" Wright asked him.

"I know two things," Daniels answered firmly. "One, it's way too early to be asking that question. And two, it doesn't matter what *I* think—you're the one who's thinking of giving it a try."

Wright seemed to have no difficulty accepting Daniels' response. The librarian reached for the volume of Miller and Starr that, according to its spine, contained the chapter on adverse possession. As the two men sat with it at the table, Daniels said, "I gotta warn you, this is some very heavy reading." He turned to the beginning of the chapter, where they looked at the detailed table of contents. "See what I mean?"

"I know how to *read*," Wright joked, but he also sounded a little miffed.

"Of course, of course. But reading laws, and books about laws, is very demanding. This stuff is incredibly dense."

He decided to share some of what he'd learned working for Simonson, both to serve as an introduction for Wright and to give him a sense of the complexity. "So," he began, "your idea of 'taking it over yourself'—and with all respect I'm not sure you completely know what you mean when you put it that way—it's only one of several pieces, several different things you have to do if you're gonna become legal owner of that parcel. That's your goal, your plan, right?"

"Right. At least until I convince myself it's impossible, or not worth my effort and time."

Skimming the table of contents, Daniels saw words he was looking for in some of the sub-chapter titles. "The law says your possession has be 'hostile' and 'notorious,'" he explained. "I don't have the list memorized, and I know there are some other adjectives on it, too. The point is, you need to understand what those terms mean, legally speaking, and then for you to succeed you have to be able to prove, in court, that they're true. Plus, and this is maybe the most important thing, the person trying to gain adverse possession has to pay the property taxes for five years in a row, and during that time the owner *isn't* doing that."

Daniels studied Wright's face, trying to gauge his response to this information. Wright had always struck him as intelligent, therefore presumably capable of reading Miller and Starr on his own. Still, the librarian expected lots of questions would arise from Wright's research and, as usual, he felt willing and ready to help a patron find answers.

"I think I'll leave you here with the book," he said then, "so you can see what you can figure out on your own. But before I do that, I have a suggestion to make."

"What's that?"

"Go to the recorder's office so you can get more information about the property, and to the tax collector to find out about the tax payments. You know where those are?"

"I'm guessing they're not in this building, or you would've said 'Go to the second floor' or something like that."

"Right. They're in a building where a lot of county offices are now. They used to be here in the courthouse, but about twenty years ago almost everything was moved except the courts. Anyway, what do you think of my suggestion? If you want to go to that other building, I can tell you how to get there. Or maybe save that for later and what you want to do right now is read."

"Why don't I read first? Then I'll let you know how that's going and also find out where the other place is."

"OK." Daniels returned to the front desk, where he had a few other things to do. He pulled a couple of folders out from the top-left drawer in the desk but at the same time kept recalling Wright's offer to share with him an idea he said nobody else knew about. It struck him as odd. No matter, he figured, if Wright really was going to seek adverse possession, at some point he'd have to tell *lots* of people.

Before long Wright came to ask for paper to take notes on, and Daniels supplied him with a few sheets from a stack beside the copy machine. Fifteen minutes later he asked if he could borrow the volume of Miller and Starr. Daniels explained the library policy of restricting borrowing to lawyers. Then Wright wasn't heard from for three-quarters of an hour, at which time he came forward again, evidently on his way out.

"How'd that go?" Daniels asked.

"Good. It's what I need to know, for sure. And for sure you were also right about reading that stuff—heavy duty! Can't stay any longer today, though. Lots more errands to run."

As Wright stood near the front desk, slightly rearranging his clothes and belongings in advance of his exit, Daniels noticed the scrap paper switching from hand to hand; the sheets were partly rolled but there was some writing on them.

"And how do I get to that building you told me about?" Wright asked.

"You know your way around Grant City?"

"I've been here enough times to get the general layout, but I . . . . Look," he went on,"maybe you'd draw me a map." He unrolled one piece of paper from the others and flattened it against the clear plastic sheet that covered the large calendar on the desk. Daniels drew lines to mark the courthouse and downtown as a starting point, but then

126

because he needed to show how to get to a fairly distant place, he had to make sure his lines didn't run off the paper. When he finished this map he explained it to Wright, who thanked him enthusiastically.

"Going there today?" Daniels inquired.

"Don't see how I have time for it." He rolled the papers up tighter, then stuffed them into a back pocket of his jeans. "Seems like you're gonna see a lot more of me," he said with a grin as he left.

Considering simply the driving distance from those remote parcels to Grant City, in addition to what struck Daniels as a very long shot at gaining adverse possession, he actually didn't assume he'd see Wright again. The matter had sufficiently captured his interest, though, whether Wright returned or not, that in some of his ample spare time he fetched the bulky volume of Miller and Starr and studied it on his own. He'd observed during other forays into the real estate bible that just about every sentence in it ended with a superscript, which in turn referred to a host of court decisions. He wondered whether Wright knew what to make of the standard system of case citations, which was basic knowledge for a law librarian but not necessarily for someone else. Then he imagined explaining the citation system to Wright so that if he wanted to, Wright could look up cases on his own. In the meantime, as he read, Daniels just glanced at some of the case titles, including one from 1923 with the wonderful name *Kafka v Bozio*.

He realized there was a great deal more than he'd learned, let alone investigated, when he worked for Simonson. For one thing, there was a not obvious

127

boundary between adverse possession and what Miller and Starr, quoting past distinctions, called "prescriptive title." For another, Daniels had been correct when he told Wright the list of adjectives he'd named was incomplete, since "actual" and "exclusive" belonged on it, too. And among the actions required of the tentative adverse possessor was one to "give notice" to the property owner of record.

His study gave him fuller understanding not only of what the law said but crucially of what Wright would have to do and prove. In one minefield of a sentence Miller and Starr acknowledged, "Whether the actual occupation and dominion of an adverse possessor is sufficiently open and notorious to constitute notice to the owner is a question of fact in each case and depends on the particular land, its condition, locality, and appropriate use." The whole business struck Daniels as even more tortuous than he'd thought, making the outcome of any particular initiative like Wright's impossible to predict.

The next time Wright strode into the library he was soon telling the librarian about the "far out" visits he'd made to the recorder and tax collector. "Pretty strange at the recorder's. They've got these huge books with maps of every parcel in the county. I was able to find mine, and then I was studying the one I told you about. It's bigger than I thought. And it's owned by some guy named Wilson who lives in Gilroy. No wonder he doesn't come up here."

"What did you find out about the taxes?"

"Wilson paid them four years ago but hasn't paid since."

"Are you prepared to . . . can you afford to pay them?"

"We'll have to see about that. Almost for sure in a couple of months." He fished out the scrap paper from last time and continued, "I've still got a bunch of questions, and I hope you've got time to help me understand this stuff better."

"Happy to try," said Daniels. "I'll be with you shortly." He returned to some papers on his desk, while Wright went back to Miller and Starr.

When Daniels joined him, Wright said, "It's clear to me you set me up with the right book. So I thank you for that. But it just doesn't seem to tell me what to do."

"Can't say I'm surprised to hear you say that. This notion of adverse possession didn't just come up for the first time yesterday. And at least in theory, it can apply all over, not just in remote places like yours. Besides, a lawyer might be on either side of a case, trying to get adverse possession *for* a client or defending a client *against* it."

Daniels asked to see Wright's paper, then read the notes on it. Finding one that included the word "hostile," he zeroed in on that term, first as it was explained in the text, reading Miller and Starr aloud, line by difficult line. Then he pointed to the bottom of the page. "You see all these— they're at the bottom of every page really—they refer to court cases. To get the whole idea you have to look up the cases and read what they said, in whatever year they were decided." As he'd anticipated, Daniels proceeded to give Wright a lesson on case citations.

Wright asked more questions, and Daniels used the book to try to answer them. As they sat together he had a somewhat different impression of Wright than before, but no particular way to name the difference. A point arrived when he somehow felt he should step back, and as a nearly unconscious signal, he pushed his chair away from the table.

"I could use some more of your time," Wright said, in a tone Daniels thought was different too: more insistent, less currying of favor.

"I hear you," the librarian insisted. "But I hope you understand I have to draw lines. You have to do most of the work yourself, you know, and you can see how much there is to do. I don't mean I won't help with specifics. Because I will."

Wright sat back in his chair. "Shit," he muttered.

Aware of the cold water his message had dumped on the man, Daniels immediately added, "Look, no matter what, you're doing the right thing to learn as much as you can. But since on top of all of this you have to go to court, it *does* seem to me you need a lawyer."

Wright was thinking it over. After a long pause he said, "We don't have one."

"That doesn't mean there isn't somebody out there who'd take your case." Now the librarian paused. "Of course, like the taxes, it's gonna cost you."

"We're not worrying about that."

Daniels returned to the front desk, wondering whether Wright returned to Miller and Starr. Ten minutes later he had his answer as Wright stood in front of him, clearly about to leave. "I guess that'll do it for today," he said. "I need to think about where I'm going with this. But I *will* come back."

"Sounds good."

Daniels hesitated before he went on. "You know, I couldn't help noticing you said 'we' a couple of times. I thought you told me nobody else even knows about your idea. So I got used to hearing only 'I'."

With a booming guffaw Wright answered, "Yeah, I knew you'd pick up on that. There's more to the story, see. Really my idea started out as a way to get something for Sheila—my lady—as a wedding present. We've been more or less together for years, see, but she lives in town. Well, six months ago I convinced her we should get married and she should come out to live with me."

"That's great!" Daniels chimed in (not sure why he'd taken that tone, but not regretting it).

"I also thought it would be great if she could have her own space to hang out in. My house does have enough room for both of us, but it's gonna be a little tight, especially in winter."

"Does she know you've been coming here? That you went to those county offices?"

"Mm, yes and no. She came to Grant City with me the last time I came to the library, and I told her I was coming up here. We both had tons of things to do in town. But the day I went to the county building, and then today, I came by myself. My idea has been to keep it a secret—including from her. At this point, though, it seems like back to the drawing board." The tone of Wright's last thought wasn't as discouraged as it might have been. Seemingly restored to his familiar upbeat mood, he told Daniels, "You've been a huge help to me. And I want you to know I appreciate it." He extended his powerful hand across the desk for the librarian to grip and shake. Then he left.

Wright came back two weeks later, at which point he wanted to consult with Daniels about finding a lawyer.

131

The librarian motioned for him to take the chair at the desk with the library-business computer. Wright explained that he'd confided in a friend, talked the issues over with him, then decided that no matter how much he learned about adverse possession, he'd never know how to navigate the formalities of court.

It seemed right to Daniels not to make any specific recommendations of an attorney for Wright to contact, but at the same time he silently thought of a few names. The case didn't strike Daniels as one a lawyer would take on a contingency basis; because it wasn't unmistakably about money, he guessed Wright would have to pay by the billable hour. Even so, he imagined, there were probably attorneys who wouldn't charge for a first meeting.

They looked together at "Attorneys" in the thin Manzanita County telephone book, narrowing the search to a few categories, then finding under those a few names. At the same time Daniels knew that, categories notwithstanding, in order to make a living many lawyers didn't specialize, doing a variety of business no matter what their alleged expertise.

"Know anything about this guy?" Wright asked regarding a lawyer named King.

"I'd say . . . I know enough to tell you to keep looking."

Wright gave him a funny look then returned to the listings. "What about Michael Pearson?"

"Never heard of him. Which means you may as well give him a try." The number had a local prefix, and Daniels let Wright use the library's phone, stepping away as he dialed.

When the librarian came back Wright said, "I didn't talk to Pearson, just his secretary. But she said I could have a very short meeting with him today, at 1:30. And she said it wouldn't cost me!"

"There you go," said Daniels. "That's something." Pearson's office was in the downtown of Grant City. The time was 11:25. "You need to get anything ready for your meeting? Obviously, if you want to, you can go back to Miller and Starr. Or, I don't know, you can go have lunch someplace. But you don't need me to tell you that. The only thing is, when you're done with your meeting I'll have left the library for the day. So I'm not sure when I'll see you again."

Wright headed toward the rear of the library. "I don't want to get bogged down in that book again, but maybe it'd be a good idea to make a few notes, to get my head together for meeting with this Pearson."

Daniels nodded but said nothing. He'd been remembering Frederick Simonson and wondering whether Wright might get any help from him. For the moment it seemed better that Pearson's name had surfaced. A few minutes before noon he went back to check and saw that Miller and Starr was on the table but closed. "You doing OK?" he asked.

"Yeah. This was a good way to use my time. I've written down a bunch of stuff so I don't go meet this guy and not know what to say."

"Sounds good. I'm gonna be taking off. One of the assistants will be here for the rest of the afternoon. Also want to make sure you know how to get to Pearson's office."

"Thanks. Yeah, where is it?"

Daniels was easily able to explain without a map this time, since the office was just three blocks from the courthouse. "Hey," he added, "I've been wanting to show you a quote I came across." He reached for Miller and Starr. "To me this is a riot. Some judge really sent everything back to where 'hostile' and 'notorious' mean what we expect them to mean."

Finding the right page, he read the quote: "The adverse possessor must unfurl his flag on the land, and keep it flying, so that the owner may see, if he will, that an enemy has invaded his domains, and planted the standard of conquest."

"Whoa!" Wright exclaimed. "I see why it jumped out at you! Sounds like the history of so-called civilization."

"Agreed," Daniels said. "And good luck."

Daniels didn't see Wright for months. He'd been curious about the meeting with Pearson but made nothing of the fact he never got any report. Then one morning Wright crossed the threshold and proclaimed, "Long time no see!"

A moment later the librarian said, "So. Last time I saw you you were headed for a meeting with . . ."

"Pearson," Wright cut in. "Nice guy. Spent almost half an hour with me. What he said was something I really should have seen myself. Remember I told you what I found out at the tax collector?"

"Help me."

"Well, Wilson—the guy that owns the parcel—hasn't paid any property tax in four years. But I haven't paid for *any* years. So, what Pearson said was, and this is what I should have realized: if I want to go for adverse possession I better get started on the taxes, 'cuz it won't be for a long time till I can make any claim."

"At least it's good to be clear on that. So where do things stand now?"

Wright launched his hearty laugh. "Yeah, it's been so long since I've come in here you wouldn't know, would you."

"True. I'm not in the loop. Know what?"

"For one thing, pretty quickly I decided it's not worth it to start paying, the taxes or the lawyer. But for another, Sheila changed *her* mind: we're not getting married. She says she'd rather stay in town. But we're still 'partners,' if you know what I mean."

Daniels thought he knew, but the expression on his face didn't commit.

"You know, like, *business* partners—in the *industry*."

Now, though he didn't say anything, Daniels did understand.

"And besides," Wright went on, "probably just as well *not* to own that parcel. Sheila and I've been growing dope on it for years anyway. Seems like we should just keep on keeping on."

Daniels had occasional conversations with Eduardo Wolheim, the multilingual court interpreter who came fairly often to Grant City from his home in another county. When there was sufficient need for his services he'd commute for the entire day—he did the same thing on other days in other counties. But this schedule didn't mean he was continuously busy, so he'd take breaks in the law library.

Besides his thick walrus mustache and cosmopolitan air, another distinctive trait was his accent, which in turn explained his hybrid name: he'd been born in Argentina, of immigrant German parents. When there was enough time he was talkative and liked to tell stories of his life. For instance, despite foreign birth he'd become active in the politics of his small California town, even serving as its mayor for a time.

It was routine for Daniels' conversations with all his visitors to be interrupted by an unfamiliar someone needing law-library help. On one occasion when he'd been chatting with Wolheim, a woman came in who wanted to obtain a subpoena but had no understanding of what such a thing might entail. She said her public defender wasn't assisting her and was unavailable when she tried to contact him— a complaint Daniels heard all too frequently. During part of his interaction with her, the woman thanked him for a compliment he didn't really intend to make; in other words, what she heard she misunderstood. In any case, he managed to provide her with forms he thought she'd need, and he felt gratified to assist her.

Wolheim overheard some of their conversation, and after she departed the two men resumed talking, including about her. The librarian recalled later that it was he who had first described the woman as "ding-y," but he believed he'd chosen the word objectively, impartially. When Wolheim used the same word, however, the interpreter seemed to mean something quite different by it, his definition colored by weariness dealing in courthouses with the mentally ill.

The Assistant

FOR MANY YEARS prior to Henry Daniels' time working there, the Manzanita County Law Library was partly an arm of the Manzanita County Public Library. They were never in the same building but were joined bureaucratically.

That universally familiar institution the public library was a department of the County of Manzanita. The law library, open to the public but highly specialized, was a creation of the State of California. The public library's main branch (there were smaller ones elsewhere) was in a stand-alone building in downtown Grant City. A hundred years earlier it had been a very small Carnegie library, in a handsome building of that era; expansion in the 1960s moved it to a bland but much more spacious structure at a different site. The law library was a few blocks away from each of those locations, inside the courthouse, which had a long and more complicated history of its own.

Early on, it was decided to classify law library employees (including the librarian) as employees of the public library, in the category of "part-time extra help." One part of the law librarian's job was to deliver invoices and time sheets, amounting to a very small number each month, to the public library. There a woman bundled them with that library's much more extensive paperwork, and in turn she delivered them to the department where all the county's bills were paid. The public library charged the law library nothing for this service, and for years it was a stable arrangement.

Law library assistants, as "part-time extra help," got a low hourly wage and no benefits. Their position being so limited, they typically had another job—or even more than one. For many years nearly all of them also worked part-time at the public library (though not all labeled "extra help"). When there was an opening for a law library assistant, it wasn't surprising that part-timers at the public library were the first to learn about it; then one of them seeking more paid work would apply and get the job. Sometimes there were two, sometimes three assistants working regular hours, up to only ten or twelve hours a week. Plus there were one or two more not on the schedule but available to fill in.

During the first ten years that Edward Donovan was director, the assistants were all women. Then Daniels was hired. His first time crossing the threshold had come when he was trying to be a paralegal. Soon, though, instead of further pursuit of that career, he became an assistant at the library, (and, once again, a part-time teacher).

Donovan had previously retired after a long career as an attorney, in Southern California. His wife, Ellie, was a librarian, and after his retirement he went back to school to become one also. They were living in San Diego but at some point decided to return to his Northern California roots, both eventually finding work in Manzanita County. She became reference librarian at the main branch of the public library and he found his niche in the courthouse. Daniels worked as an assistant for seven or eight years before Donovan, by then a widower, sold his home and retired for good. It was on his recommendation that

Daniels was promoted to become his successor, (better paid but still "part-time extra help").

Almost as soon as Daniels was in charge, the law library faced what at first seemed an administrative disaster. The head of the public library came to a meeting of the Board of Trustees to announce that, due to its budget crisis, her library could no longer provide the old services at no cost. It would now be $15,000 a year. Daniels knew enough about the law library's financial condition to receive this news as a devastating blow. But then, in bold rapid response to it, the Board declared independence: thenceforward the librarian and assistants would be employees of the Board itself, with Daniels as director having more responsibilities. Before long a new regime was successfully in place.

As it had for many years, occasional turnover in the ranks of the assistants continued, and when the need arose Daniels continued the practice of hiring public library part-timers for the job. A break from this tradition arose, though, when word of mouth brought forward a woman named Valerie. She had no connection to the public library, in fact no connection to libraries of any kind, according to a resumé heavy on selling women's clothes. Petite and, not surprisingly, well dressed, she accented stylish outfits with colorful scarves. The librarian also inhaled a strong perfume.

Over the course of his own years as an assistant, Daniels had demonstrated his aptitude to Donovan and built up skills at assisting patrons of the law library. Nonetheless, he thought the basic work of the assistant was uncomplicated: operate the copy machine; handle small amounts of money; help people log on to a handful of computer programs; of course be courteous and friendly. One daily task, which every assistant seemed to enjoy as a break, was to descend to the courthouse basement in mid-afternoon to collect the library's mail. Another was to announce late in the day, if anyone was still using the library then, that it would shortly be closing. Daniels' quick assessment was that Valerie could do these things, and because he wasn't inclined to search for someone else, he added her to the staff.

Over the course of many years one of the most frequent visitors to the library was a man who knew — or confidently thought he did—a great deal about the law, even though he wasn't a lawyer. Wallace Vaughn when he came there was entirely self-directed: he knew where the various resources and reference works were shelved, and he knew how to pursue detailed legal research on his own. In the course of many hours of concentrated study he accumulated small stacks of books, eventually carrying armloads of them to the copy machine, which he knew very well how to operate. Consequently he required no help from Daniels, other than for the latter to accept payment, typically for a very large number of copies.

Coexistent with this silent and highly focused demeanor was an extraordinarily talkative side of the man, which Vaughn nearly always displayed upon entering and exiting the library. Over the course of their interactions the law librarian came to know him as extremely outgoing, with a confident spirit, but also garrulous. He needed no prompting to shift gears and suddenly deliver extended monologues, Daniels serving as an audience of one. And audience it virtually was, as Vaughn would be in self-

141

labeled "standup" mode, delivering jokes and shtick he said he'd written and performed professionally. He transformed himself into a nightclub comic, complete with gimmicks of gesture, voice, and timing—none of which the librarian found very funny.

In nearly nonstop patter he veered between this standup and flows of commentary about his legal pursuits, the latter changing over time. Years earlier, before Daniels became an assistant, Vaughn had triumphed in a lawsuit and been awarded $40,000. With unquestionable generosity he'd donated all the proceeds, half to a health center near his home in eastern Manzanita County, half to the perennially needy law library, which had been of so much help to him in his research. Such largesse gained him seemingly permanent good will and made his quirks easier to ignore.

Something that struck Daniels about the man was that he invariably made reference to the number of pages in his filings, as if the sheer amount of paper was a reliable indicator of invincible argument. Also, even on days he wasn't scheduled to go to court—where he always represented himself—Vaughn was exceptionally well dressed, in high-quality suit and tie. The source of his money was an unknown, though occasionally he mentioned a wealthy foundation in San Francisco. His neatly barbered hair was dyed a faint orange.

One other aspect of Vaughn's personality surfaced occasionally, a tendency to flirt with the assistants. Since Daniels normally departed shortly after an assistant arrived to work for the rest of the day, he rarely observed this. But there had been several times when Vaughn made an approach to one or another of the women while the librarian was still there. Briefly in his comic mode he'd tell a joke, something that Daniels, overhearing, considered slightly off-color. Had it been told to him alone, he'd have let it go as of a piece with all Vaughn's material. But being directed to a woman, he thought, cast it in a different light. Indeed, in the immediate aftermath of one of Vaughn's odd attempts to be funny, Janet, a woman Daniels knew from long acquaintance to be quite modest and proper, wore an offended frown as she wordlessly turned and walked away.

Vaughn had been about to exit; Daniels deliberately waited for him to leave. As director, he'd gradually internalized his overall responsibility for the library but also recognized within himself a special protectiveness regarding the assistants. Now, although he considered saying something to Janet, the situation felt awkward, and so, at least for the moment, he chose not to. Descending the stairs to exit the courthouse himself, he reflected on his inability to control what happened in the library when he wasn't there.

When Daniels agreed to take on Valerie as an assistant, she explained that she'd very recently moved to Grant City and was in the process of looking for a place to live. For the time being she was staying with an elderly aunt, as well as to some degree being her caregiver. Once she could find a small, affordable place of her own, she said, she would continue to look in on her aunt.

Having listened to Wallace Vaughn expound at length on various legal topics, Daniels knew that he regarded himself as a particular expert on real estate. One afternoon not long after Valerie began as an assistant, Vaughn, in silent mode, was working in the rear of the library. He'd come in during the morning and stayed well past the time Daniels left for the day. It was impossible for Daniels later to reconstruct what occurred in his absence, but Vaughn evidently engaged Valerie in conversation of some kind. Daniels learned about it the next morning when she telephoned the library. Sounding upset, she said she felt she needed to report the incident because she somehow didn't feel quite right about it. Vaughn had approached her when it was time to pay for the copies he'd made, and in making general conversation she let him know she was looking for a place to live. He proceeded immediately to provide her with advice on the dos and don'ts of renting, plus a great deal of information about the local real estate market.

"I've been having a hard time finding a place," she told Daniels, "so I really appreciated that he was taking a special interest like that." She said Vaughn identified some real estate offices and wrote down some numbers for her to call. "But then he asked me *if I'd like him to show me around*, after I got off work. Right then my alarm bells went off: I told him no thank you. He took that okay, I guess, and wished me luck."

Not only did Daniels' whole dossier on Vaughn flip open with this news, but also a nearly empty folder on Valerie. With her still on the line, he felt a strong need to say something, but he wasn't sure what; he was unwilling to share his private opinion of Vaughn, nor did it seem appropriate to deliver a lecture to a woman he barely knew about how to conduct her life. A fallback strategy emerged: he talked to her about working in the law library, that it was very important to develop skills for listening to people and be willing to help them, but at the same time to draw boundaries. Since she'd just begun working there, she replied, she realized there were things she needed to know. She thanked him and, as if to reinforce the lesson, repeated the word "boundaries" several times.

One afternoon a few weeks later as he was leaving the courthouse, Daniels saw Valerie and Vaughn enter Schindler's together. They didn't see him. It was none of his business, of course, but he naturally wondered what was going on.

Although the library was occasionally busy, there was a lot of "down time," particularly for the assistants. With that in mind, Daniels told them to feel free to access a computer for personal use. Ruth, a veteran of the public library, always brought a book to read (usually a detective novel), so he guessed she didn't get online at all. In the past Janet had shared enough about herself for him to realize she was trying hard to build self-esteem. Sometimes she brought a book in that category, at others she was studying something on a monitor. Valerie upon her arrival went immediately to log on; Daniels didn't know or care much where she went on the net, but a time or two he glimpsed images of womenswear.

Unlike Janet and Ruth, who routinely arrived in the library five or so minutes before they were "on the clock," Valerie appeared right at the time when she was supposed to begin work. By arriving early, the other assistants created a few minutes for conversation with Daniels about whatever the day's business might entail. In contrast, by arriving when she did, Valerie subtly forced him to "stay late" if there was to be any such conversation. It wasn't at all that he minded staying late—something he'd do routinely if he was helping someone—as that he felt it said something about her attitude. He knew he took his own job seriously in a manner unreasonable to expect from the assistants. Even so, he realized, he was distinguishing Valerie from the others.

A very important task that needed to be done several times a year was to insert update pages into the library's multivolume reference sets. These were printed by the publisher and sent in large cartons to every subscriber. The tiny mailroom in the courthouse basement flashed a major signal when, instead of there being nothing, or just one or two envelopes, at the bottom of the plastic bin marked "Law Library," it was filled to far past overflowing with eight, ten or a dozen of these cartons, each filled with many hundreds of sheets of very thin, three-hole-punched paper.

Daniels in his years as Donovan's assistant had gained lots of experience carrying out this task. It involved using a pamphlet titled *FILING INSTRUCTIONS* that came with the shipment, in order to know which pages in the volumes were to be removed and which pages in the cartons were to replace them. When the work was under way, the pagination in the volumes, which reflected years and years of previous updates (and with each new insert altered the page numbers still more), was extremely complicated; without sharp focus it was easy to screw up. From dozens of hours of doing it Daniels knew the work was brain-numbingly tedious, yet he'd repeatedly experienced an odd satisfaction by maintaining the concentration it required.

The first time updates arrived shortly after Valerie began work as an assistant, the librarian was glad to spend a lot of time showing her how to follow the filing instructions. In the course of doing so, he made explicit that this was a very important job, on which he and all the assistants were expected to work until all the updates had been inserted. At the same time he said he didn't want anyone to focus so intensely or so long as to give herself a headache.

Several different reference sets were updated in the same manner, the monster on the shelves being *California Forms of Pleading and Practice*, which filled fifty-three massive blue binders, each one numbered as a volume and within each containing many separately numbered chapters. The publisher, Lexis-Nexis, sent cartons of updates for the entire set three or four times a year. The standard practice Daniels inherited and taught was to put a check mark in the filing instructions next to individual pages in the various chapters as he proceeded, and then next to the volume number after all the updates for that volume had been inserted. This system provided a clear way for the next person who would continue the updating to know where to begin. As a quiet means of knowing whether an assistant had spent adequate time at the task, before he left at mid-day Daniels took note of the current volume number and looked again the following morning, to see what progress had been made.

Some months after the initial training from him, and having gained additional experience dealing with other updates, Valerie was the assistant scheduled to work one afternoon. The filing instructions and a volume of *California Forms of Pleading and Practice* were on the front desk when she arrived. Daniels had put a check mark beside the number of the previous volume in the filing instructions, meaning that he had completed updating it. As was her habit, the assistant arrived almost exactly at the time she was supposed to begin work, and as was also her habit, she carried her large handbag to the desk where one

147

of the computers sat. On this day there actually was no need for the librarian to engage in other than "How are you?" pleasantries with her; he assumed the volume on the desk and the cartons on the floor made entirely clear that she had library work to do.

The next morning he unlocked the door, expecting to begin the library day as usual. But when he saw a volume of *California Forms of Pleading and Practice* on the desk and, lifting it up, discovered that the number on its spine proved it was the same one he'd left there the previous day, he was furious.

It was not uncommon for the assistants to communicate with each other about switching afternoons, in order to accommodate someone's need (or unstated wish?) to be absent. The large-scale calendar grid on the front desk was used for the purpose of keeping the schedule current, evident to anyone with a need to check it. Daniels was already aware but now, glancing at the calendar, was reminded that because of a switch Valerie was scheduled to work again later that same day.

The emotion that flared in him when he made his discovery, though it subsided slightly, remained with him through the morning, in large part because he knew he'd be seeing her at midday. It was definitely not all right with him that she'd spent no time on the inserts, yet he wasn't at all sure how he wanted to communicate this to her. During the morning he found himself "rehearsing" for an exchange with her—but for what sort of exchange he had no script.

Something else he pondered was whether to continue with the inserts himself. He did have time to do some, but if he advanced into another volume or beyond, the fact of her not having done her job would seem, he thought, less stark. Even having to think about such things further stoked his anger. Ultimately, though not without also feeling petty and vindictive, he chose not to do any more of them. When Valerie entered the library, advancing as usual to a computer and setting down her handbag, it appeared to him she was altogether oblivious. She walked casually to the front desk to check in with him. By that point the tension within him was wound so tight it was difficult for him to speak.

"Valerie," he began, "*Why didn't you do any of these inserts?!*"

"What?" she responded. "What are you talking about?"

"These inserts," he said, waving his hand toward the cartons. "This binder . . . it's the same one I left here on the desk yesterday, the last time I saw you." His voice was under even more pressure. "You had *all afternoon* to work on this, and I can see you didn't put in even one page!"

By no means apologizing, but rather cutting him off with anger of her own she said, "Excuse me! I don't know why you're speaking to me that way. What's gotten you so stirred up? If you have a problem, I insist that you write me a note or call me at home to discuss it—not like this!"

Taken slightly aback by her response, Daniels was still convinced there was no good explanation for what she hadn't done. "We're here right now," he answered. "So I want to talk right now. I don't know, maybe my tone was wrong—maybe. But you *must* know what I'm talking about. Do you or don't you?"

At that point she turned and left the library, without another word.

Daniels, his thoughts sputtering, wasn't inclined to aim words at her back, so he didn't. Meanwhile it was time for him to leave for the day, and he didn't want to await her return. As he was thinking about how to handle this weird situation—he could leave and lock the door, he knew she had a key, but maybe she hadn't taken it with her—she reappeared, wordlessly advancing to "her" computer. Then Daniels walked out.

A stalemate of sorts ensued. The insert job was completed by all three assistants and Daniels. He said no more about their confrontation, and Valerie showed no sign that it had affected anything.

A separate incident took place shortly after that, but the potential conflict in it occurred completely apart from Valerie, though she was again Daniels' focus. She announced to him one day that she intended to use some of the "Vacation Time" shown on her paystub. Never having noticed such a category on the stub of his own check, nor ever having observed any other assistant do such a thing, the librarian in truth wasn't aware that "Vacation Time" for law library employees even existed.

For many years, in order to limit payroll expense, it had been library practice (probably established long before Donovan's tenure, then continued by Daniels) to have no more than one employee working at a time. If someone needed to be away, the person made arrangements with someone else to work those hours, and any time a situation like that arose, as far back as Daniels could remember, the absent employee simply forfeited payment. In other words, for each hour the library was open only one person was paid.

Now, however, assuming the library would be open for its usual number of hours, Valerie's decision to use "Vacation Time" meant *two* people would be paid, a sub as

150

well as herself. Besides violating the library's unwritten "policy," this ran afoul of Daniels' personal work ethic. It was highly doubtful she had any such rarefied philosophy; instead, he figured, she brought with her from other jobs the conventional notion that, once having worked a requisite length of time, employees routinely accrued "Vacation Time."

The librarian fretted about this. He was reluctant to discuss it with anyone, concerned that he would seem simply miserly. It continued to nag at him, though, until one day he researched state law, eventually locating the website of California's Department of Industrial Relations. He studied the regulations carefully, which appeared to confirm that the paystub information was consistent with current labor law. The DIR website showed the department had offices in various cities around the state, and so to fully answer his doubts he called the one in Redding. Sure enough, according to the knowledgeable person on the other end of the line, even an employee who'd been on the job for as short a time, and worked as few hours a week, as Valerie was entitled to "Vacation Time."

Daniels knew he had to let the issue go yet remained of divided mind: he supported progressive laws that insured workers' rights, but he resented Valerie. As time passed he tried not to find fault with her, and she gave him no more reason to. He could see she was intelligent and capable; he lacked the ability to forgive and forget.

Daniels continued to see Wallace Vaughn from time to time, in the library but also occasionally when he walked past the open doors of the office of the Clerk of the Court and spotted Vaughn filing legal papers. By now it had been many years since Vaughn prevailed in the case that enabled him to make his generous donation. He'd moved on to other lawsuits, in none of which, as far as Daniels could tell, had he triumphed. The persistent non-attorney continued his voluminous research and copying, and occasionally his monologues revealed some information about what he was working on. To the librarian it appeared that Vaughn kept being rebuffed in court, since he kept referring to appeals he was lodging, appeals of decisions that had gone against him.

Having at various times looked into guidebooks on filing an appeal, Daniels knew it was a painstaking procedure, which, if not done carefully, would lead the appellate court to refuse even to consider the case. So he was impressed by Vaughn's apparent knowledge of procedure, but at the same time he wondered why Vaughn kept having no success.

Because Daniels lived not far from Grant City's downtown, he usually walked to the courthouse, entering through its southern door. He counted as a very small but pleasant "perk" the fact that the security guards knew him and routinely waved him around the metal detector. The job of the guards appeared to be extremely boring; at the direction of their crew chief and for a little variety they rotated from time to time, shuttling to work also at the east entrance. The chief was a stout, very friendly guy named Frank. Besides bantering with regular employees and familiar visitors (also paying proper deference to judges), he made it his business to know a lot about what was going on in the building.

He knew Daniels by name: "How ya doin', Henry," he'd say. But they'd never had any substantial conversation until one day Frank asked, "Havin' any trouble with this guy Vaughn?"

Daniels answered no.

Frank went on to tell him security was keeping its eye on the library's distinctive patron. "I guess he was bugging one of the clerks enough he got reported to court administration. Then the head man up there told *me.* Lemme know if he's making any trouble—we know he's in your library a lot."

Daniels nodded, to thank the chief and to show he understood.

It was a few weeks after that when some sort of shouting must have burst loudly from the law library into the hallway outside it and resounded in the building's open stairwell. What exactly transpired Daniels never knew, since he wasn't working at the time. But piecing together facts he did know, the event occurred fairly close to 4:00, at which time the only people in the library were Vaughn and Valerie. For some reason she must have left abruptly, and as she did she emitted a loud sound, not words so much as a kind of cry. Her yell mobilized a sheriff's deputy, a uniformed officer at that time assigned to stand just inside Courtroom E, across the hall. Daniels speculated that the deputy must have felt he was being called away from duty vastly more important, for after observing that the assistant was apparently unharmed, his rapid action was to order Vaughn to leave and Valerie to lock up.

When Daniels arrived for work the next morning, he knew nothing about this incident. But upon opening the library's email a short time later, he found a message from Wallace Vaughn, which was a lengthy formal complaint against the library, its Board of Trustees, Henry Daniels, and various others named as defendants. Even though sent to the inbox, it was a polished draft in legal language— Vaughn must have spent hours on it—almost ready for transferring to proper legal paper and filing as a lawsuit.

It was hard on the librarian's eyes to read the densely worded document on the monitor; after a while, confident that he got the gist of Vaughn's argument, he skimmed to the end. It alleged that the library had changed one of its rules without notice to patrons, namely, the time each day when it would close. Vaughn offered proof by declaring that the assistant working the previous afternoon had altered the schedule, forcing him to end his work earlier than the time to which he was long accustomed.

The librarian was considering options for reacting to this bizarre development when a deputy crossed the threshold. He was tall and blond, with the upper body of a linebacker as well as holstered weapons at his waist. At first he looked beyond Daniels to determine whether others were in the room. Then, seeing none, he said curtly, "You seen that guy, what's his name, Vaughn?"

"No, I haven't."

"You know what happened in here yesterday?"

"I'm just starting to find out a little about it. He sent the library an email."

"I had to kick him out. Don't really know what was going on—something with that woman who works here. You should talk to security." Without further word the deputy turned and left.

Daniels continued thinking about what to do as he followed the routines of every morning. He made up his mind to call Valerie.

"Hello?" she answered.

"Valerie? It's Henry, from the library." Thinking she might respond, he paused, but she didn't, so he cautiously went on. "Did something happen in here yesterday afternoon?"

"Well, YES! Do you know about it? I was going to call you when I got home, but I . . . " She didn't finish.

"Something with a deputy?"

"Yes, I had to get help! He was threatening me."

"Who was?"

"You know that guy, Vaughn something."

"What do you mean he was 'threatening' you?"

"He started yelling, then he was coming toward the front desk. So I ran out! The deputy heard, and he came out of the courtroom."

"What was he yelling about?"

"Something about not being able to get his work done, I think. But honestly, I didn't understand. And he was coming toward me. He's weird!"

Daniels decided against telling Valerie about the email. He didn't recall her being named as one of the defendants, but the list did include John and Jane Does. He also felt doubts about trying to get more facts from her, especially before hearing Vaughn's version of events. So he ended the call, telling her he'd see her the following afternoon, when she was next scheduled to work.

He reread the core of Vaughn's complaint, opened other messages and dealt with them, then closed down not just the computer but the library itself. The next thing to do was to hunt down Frank, to learn what he had to say. Daniels posted a "Back in 10 Minutes" sign in the window in the door, which clicked as he shut it. Then he walked downstairs to the east entrance, where Frank was chatting with a lawyer while another guard manned the metal detector. A minute or two later the lawyer took off. Daniels approached and got a raised-eyebrows look from the chief, who asked, "So you know about yesterday?"

"Not enough," Daniels answered. "That's why I'm here. A deputy came in this morning but hardly told me anything. He said I should talk to you."

"I don't really have it straight. All I know is it involved your friend Vaughn, but also the woman who works up there, who if you ask me is a little screwy herself."

Daniels didn't respond to Frank's commentary but asked him directly, "What *do* you know?"

Frank answered the question with a question: "Is there some kind of history between those two? Best I can tell, whatever happened was building on top of something else."

"Where were you? Did you hear anything? See anything?"

"No, actually I was on the sidewalk outside the south door, on my way to the bakery."

"So how do you know about it?

"Mathis, the deputy, told one of my guys later in the day, then my guy told me when we were locking up the building. I know I'm not giving you much to go on. But I did tell you to keep an eye on that Vaughn, didn't I?"

"You did," he said glumly and went back upstairs. Daniels wasn't going to tell the chief about Vaughn's email. Nor, he thought as he reopened the library, was he going to

156

inform the Board of Trustees. He didn't ask for the problem but it was his, and he was determined to deal with it on his own.

His mind was preoccupied with the matter through the rest of the morning (and later, into the night, when during one long stretch he couldn't sleep). He had no phone number for Vaughn but realized he could have communicated by replying to the email. To say what? He didn't want to respond to Vaughn's hostile message when he was still trying to figure out what had happened   At the very least he knew he'd be speaking with Valerie again at noon next day. He said nothing about it in his brief exchange with Ruth, who, arriving with her detective novel, was there to work the afternoon.

Half-way through the next morning, matters were drastically compounded when Vaughn entered. In blue suit and red tie, he barely acknowledged Daniels and walked silently to his usual place in the rear. Glancing frequently over his shoulder at the clock, the librarian realized he'd have to approach Vaughn very soon—before Valerie arrived—to communicate about the incident and the threatened lawsuit. He wished he could know what he was going to say but had to accept near-total uncertainty. Normally he wanted the library to be busier, but on this occasion the absence of anyone else was welcome. He ordered himself to stand and walk. Vaughn looked up from his research when he sensed Daniels' approach; Daniels deliberately kept some distance between them, stopping beside shelves full of *California Appellate Reports*.

"I got your email," he began simply. "I need to know what happened the other day."

157

Right away Vaughn's voice was at high intensity: "She's telling me she's going to close up and I have to leave. I tell her, 'It's not time yet,' and she just repeats, 'Closing time.'"

"What time was it?"

"I'm not absolutely positive. Three-thirty, twenty to four. The point is, she had no business doing that! *I* should know when the library is supposed to close."

"But you also know she's got things to do at the end of the day. And that it's not fair to keep her here later than she's getting paid for."

"This wasn't about that! I'm telling you: she was putting some kind of *squeeze* on me."

"Now what makes you say that?"

"She's had it in for me the whole time she's worked here. And I happen to know she's not even a librarian. What's she even doing here? I tell you: that woman is trouble."

"She ran out into the hall, 'screaming' is what I hear. What was that about?

Vaughn was exasperated. "I don't know! I tell you, I've dealt with people like her before: she's a sociopath! I say it's too early to close, and the next thing she's out the door! Then, I couldn't believe, there's a cop!"

Knowing he wasn't close to any objective account, Daniels hesitated. "And for this you want to *sue the library*? Is that what I'm supposed to understand from the email you sent?

"That's correct. There are ways to deal with this."

"Sorry but I just don't get it. You've been using this place for years and now you want to . . . *punish* it? What would that do?"

Vaughn, staring at his hands, at first made no response but then looked up and said, "You could fire her."

A long, discouraged exhale departed Daniels' lungs. He looked up at the clock. Then, as he drew in new breath, an idea came to him. "Look, there must be a way to work this out. I want to ask you to . . . *bend* . . . a little. It seems to me the problem is something between you and her. And I can't figure out what that 'something' is. Couldn't you please just come in here when she's not working? I'll give you her schedule—she's usually here only eight hours a week. I bet you can work around that."

Vaughn evidently heard, but there was no indication of what he was thinking.

"The fact is," Daniels continued, "she's working this afternoon, she'll be here at twelve. Now I realize it's asking a lot, but it would really help if today you took off before then. Do you see? I'm trying to keep you two apart."

Vaughn stared at his hands and, uncharacteristically, said no more. He did exit around 11:45.

At noon, when Valerie arrived, Daniels felt exhausted but knew he needed to make another attempt to get the facts. First he told her Vaughn had been in earlier. Then he asked directly, "What time did you close the other day?"

Clearly, she was offended. "Why are you asking me that? What did he say?"

"Would you just answer my question? What time did you close?"

"I don't know. Do you think I watch the clock the whole time? Ten till . . . maybe quarter to four. I can't believe you're asking me this."

"I've asked around about what happened," he told her. "I can't get the story straight from anybody, and I doubt I

159

ever will." Then he explained the proposal he'd put to Vaughn.

Valerie began to protest but Daniels cut her off. "I'll tell you what I told him: the best thing for everybody will be if you two keep apart. Stay away from him!"

Ten days later Daniels was in Oliver's, a market where he occasionally shopped. On that late afternoon he intended to indulge himself by selecting from the array of olives in bulk, in the deli section. He'd anticipated reaching for a container and partially filling it with kalamatas, then with other varieties he liked. As he approached, though, he spotted Vaughn and Valerie together nearby, examining labels on bottles of red wine. Abruptly he reversed course, ending up in an aisle where he could consider dozens of brands of cookies and crackers. He could also see the store's exit. Pretending to shop he waited there. He saw the couple leave arm in arm.

Fairly frequently a middle-aged man well dressed but in casual clothes, not a suit, quietly crossed the threshold.   He barely acknowledged Daniels and proceeded to the seat furthest away from the entrance, where he spread papers and books from his briefcase on one of the tables there.   Generally he stayed several hours, working on something about which the librarian had no idea.   Perhaps his reason for coming was to access reference books; he never used a computer in the library.   When he was finished on a given morning, he'd leave as quietly as he'd come in.   He didn't avoid eye contact with Daniels but didn't smile when he made it, either.

After quite a few of these visits Daniels admitted to himself that he was curious to know the man's business, which by definition was none of his own. He was used to lawyers, quite a few of them known to him and more or less friendly in manner, using the library for their unannounced purposes.   Usually they were dressed up, for court appearances.   Something about the man, although he wasn't in a suit, suggested to Daniels that he also might be an attorney.

Daniels decided to approach the man, in the least invasive way he could, to see if he could learn more. One morning he walked back to where the man habitually sat and said, "Excuse me.   It certainly seems you don't need any help.   But I thought I'd offer it, just in case there's something you might be looking for, that I could help you find."

"No," the man, who seemed a little surprised by the offer, replied.   "I'm fine."

Daniels was not surprised. But his curiosity remained, and having come this far he said, "I hope you won't think I'm out of line for asking, but I see you come in here fairly often and it's made me wonder what you're working on."

"Uh-huh," the stranger said, acknowledging at the same time as blocking the inquiry.

The non-response had the effect on Daniels of further increasing his curiosity. Though turning and walking away seemed the "right" thing to do at that moment, somehow he was unwilling to.

"Are you an attorney?" he blurted out.

The man laughed, a sort of gasp. "What makes you think so?"

"Well, you seem to come in here fully prepared to do . . . whatever it is you're doing. And almost all the other people I see who are as independent as that are attorneys." He added hastily, "I know I could be wrong."

The man laughed again, very slightly. "Maybe you should be a detective. Yes, you're right, I am an attorney. I live in Manzanita County but I don't practice law here. In fact, I'm wrapping up my practice."

Reflexively Daniels asked, "Where's that?"

But the man replied, "I don't want to answer any more of your questions."

The way he said it wasn't rude. Daniels understood closure, and he retreated.

162

The Clerk

AT SOME POINT a man who was neither a lawyer nor a member of the public began to make regular appearances in the library. He had a Native American body type, stocky but not fat, with a broad gut. When Henry Daniels first got to know him, he wasn't sure what the man was his face looked possibly Latino. Fleshy in the cheeks and jowls; a high forehead glistening beneath not very thick hair; a slight mustache; soft brown eyes; an intelligent mouth, alternately amused and turned off.

Daniels became increasingly interested in him over time as the man, whose name was Anthony Rabano, revealed more about himself. He was a court clerk, but the office-work clothes conventional for that position didn't hang well on that body. Both his pants and shirt fit ill around his waist. Was he oblivious to the seemingly sloppy image he left in courthouse eyes? Did he care? He told the librarian how much more comfortable he was among the transient denizens of the railroad tracks a few blocks away, drinking beer in the dark, than tolerating the platitudes of his co-workers, ninety-five percent of whom were female and whose inane chitchat never failed, he said, to chirp about "Friday." The latter impression concurred with Daniels' own about many of the clerks: complacent lifers on the state's payroll, more than content to be underlings to lawyers and judges, with basically small minds.

So little transpired in the library that when Rabano came there Daniels nearly always had time to chat with him. He was indeed Native American, an enrolled member of a tribe still populous in Manzanita and the next county to the north, where his band of the tribe owned a casino. But he hadn't grown up there. He was from Oakland, and Daniels sounded him out about his experiences on the streets of that city. He'd apparently had no choice but to learn to fight, so his "knowledge" of Blacks and Latinos was gained at least partly in combat. He was under court order to pay child support to an ex of many years ago, which sorely pinched his take-home pay. There were newer women in his life as well, but each of them presented a different type of problem: one lived too far away; one had young kids; another was too reckless in the ways she drove, spent, and drank. He didn't demonstrate any reciprocal curiosity about the librarian, who didn't mind not sharing.

Rabano's attitude toward the static and oppressed situation of his life was so profoundly bleak that, as with the look of his clothing, he quite possibly didn't care in the slightest what others thought of him. Yet beneath that, Daniels sensed, were some traces of hope and efforts to change. He told the librarian that he worked a second job, trying to earn and save enough to get out of the several holes he was in. He kept an eye—a cynical one—on the eventual conclusion of the "anger management" and DUI classes he was mandated to attend, at which point he could expect to regain his suspended driver's license and no longer have to pay for the "check-in" sessions he despised. He moved from a boarding house with a cast of irritating other tenants into his own place, a short distance from the courthouse. He was proud of the discipline imposed by a new routine: going to the junior high track early every morning before work, at first to walk laps, later to run a little. Perhaps this led to his shedding a few pounds.

Why did he even have the clerk job? Daniels didn't know but speculated that some combination of counseling, financial pressure, resignation to reality, and affirmative action had landed him in it. Their conversation made evident that he was more than smart enough to do what was required. Beyond that, a further indicator of Rabano's intelligence was a dry and sly sense of humor. His mind dug below surfaces and, with sarcasm and irony, cast light on the absurdity of things. Though he was trapped within "the system," this humor voiced a kind of independence, even liberation, from it. On a bad day he sounded merely disgusted about his life and the dull world around it. But more often the librarian was encouraged to hear undaunted evidence of that wryer voice.

Daniels resisted thinking that theirs was a full-fledged friendship, since they saw each other only in the one location and at times apparently coinciding with the clerk's breaks. When Rabano came in it was nominally to use a computer; he had email to check (he had an account but no computer where he lived), and he would also visit websites that interested him—once he invited Daniels to have a look at snapshots women had posted of themselves on a match-making site. Sooner or later, more often than not, they would find time to talk. Daniels came to believe the clerk's primary reason for coming to the law library was actually conversation; he thought he was contributing to Rabano's self-improvement (while at the same time he could see that the thought flattered himself).

The semi-regular visitor had a second kind of humor, much more physical but coming perhaps from a place

165

inside him not unlike the source of his wit. For a large man, he was remarkably light on his feet. He exploited this gift by grafting it onto Daniels' habit of deep concentration, whether on library business or grading his students' papers. The clerk would sneak into the library without being noticed and then either say something behind Daniels' back—to give him a start—or suddenly be seated at a computer before the librarian even realized he'd come in. A variant of this, which Rabano did so many times it became a private joke between them, was to sneak to a spot beside the doorway where Daniels couldn't see him and then in a gangster voice grunt, "You're goin' down, Henry." Almost never would Daniels see him race past the threshold to get there, so usually it was that nutty, disembodied threat he'd hear first, announcing the clerk's imminent entrance.

Occasionally Daniels would ask how the second job was going. Rabano's answers revealed that over time it was not one but a succession of second jobs. He'd been a security guard, first at a casino, then at a bar, but for reasons he didn't volunteer these didn't work out. Obviously they were night jobs, for which he had to show up after completing full days in the courthouse. (The librarian couldn't imagine finding the energy to stay awake at them.) Later he worked at a fast-food place, not one of the big franchises but a regional operation that specialized in ribs. He was seemingly making headway there but reached a showdown moment over . . . something—he didn't explain what—and he quit. Then it was on to a drugstore chain that stayed open late. Daniels shopped there himself occasionally and knew the layout, but since he always went in the daytime he never encountered Rabano. The manager was pretty flexible about giving Rabano the schedule he needed so he could attend those mandated meetings. But in other ways, the clerk complained, the manager, a guy a lot younger and greener than himself, was "a punk."

His ongoing reports about those groups added to Daniels' overall sense of him. He was outspoken in anger management, openly critical of its format and the leader's nice-nice style, even to the point of challenging one of the other members' confessions: "I really don't care how you're doing this week," he quoted himself telling somebody, "and I don't need you to know how *I'm* doing."

Every county in the state was supposed to open a "self-help law center," and slowpoke Manzanita was finally getting around to it. This was before Daniels became law librarian; he was working part-time as an assistant to Edward Donovan, and he could easily imagine himself more challenged by his labor. Based on the job description and his experience in the law library, Daniels considered himself highly qualified for one position in the soon-to-open center. So he went for it, filling out the application form, getting letters of reference. After he submitted this packet he sat back, expecting and waiting to be summoned for an interview.

But "sat back" falsely suggests he was relaxed when in truth he wasn't. The waiting produced a case of edginess. He told Rabano about his application, and the clerk in turn told him of another clerk, a woman, who he knew had also applied. Learning he had competition made Daniels more uptight. And the woman was bilingual, a major asset compared to what he knew was the greatest weakness in his own bid for the job.

At last came the summons for an interview; his anxiety wound tighter as its date approached. One day during this intensified wait—it was right after yet another shooting rampage in the U.S.—he happened in the course of one of their conversations to ask the clerk what he thought about gun control. As usual, Rabano was sitting at the middle computer and Daniels at the library-business one nearby. Daniels had not made any explicit connection between the massacre and the subject of his question but must have assumed the link was obvious. They were proceeding on the topic, somewhat uneasily, Daniels thought—with the clerk perhaps feeling put on the spot?—when Rabano asked, "Is this about what happened in Virginia?"

"DUH!" the librarian blurted.

The clerk abruptly stood and came toward Daniels, who was leaning back in an office chair, partially blocking him. Rabano was silently headed for the exit but the librarian, in the way, for an instant felt afraid he was about to be attacked. No, the castors gave the clerk what he wanted, which was simply to move the chair. Before Daniels could fully register what was happening, Rabano was gone.

Daniels was stunned. He felt immediate and deep remorse for having provoked such a reaction. But going after Rabano to offer an apology didn't seem an option. For one thing, he considered it his responsibility to stay in the library. For another, he'd never been to Rabano's workplace, and he couldn't imagine it being somewhere he could apologize except with other clerks watching and overhearing.

So Daniels let the next few days pass, troubled but willing to wait, at best for some healing, at least for further developments. Nothing happened for quite a while. The memory of the triggering incident gnawed at him, and he missed their connection. At the same time, he felt he couldn't take much blame for . . . whatever it was. He did nothing more than think, but he did that at length: he wanted to know what Rabano's thoughts and feelings were, how he viewed that unfortunate—but, to Daniels' mind, tiny—incident, why he was now a stranger.

The date of the interview for the position at the self-help center arrived, and Daniels appeared at the prescribed time and place. He was aware that, despite his nominal ambition, some element of confidence in himself had slumped, and as he left the interview room he knew the impression he'd made was weak. Sure enough, he didn't get the job.

He knew a little bit about the routine of Rabano's job. Sometimes in the morning the clerk came upstairs to drop off mail at various offices, including the judge's office down a short hall from the law library. (The judge's secretary opened the locked door and took the mail from him.) In earlier days the clerk would often stop briefly in the library at those times, essentially to say hello; later in the morning, on his break, he'd come in and stay much longer. Several times following the miserable "DUH!" incident, from the front desk Daniels saw him pass by on that early-morning route, and they made eye contact. The librarian thought the clerk's expression contained a slight acknowledgment of him, not really a greeting but definitely nothing hostile. Nevertheless Rabano didn't stop in. And at the accustomed later hour, he was nowhere to be seen.

In the morning on his way into the courthouse, as Daniels climbed from the security entrance to the third floor; when he descended to the basement to collect the library's mail, then re-ascended; and when he went down finally a little after noon, at the end of his shift, to exit the building, he kept looking for Rabano. He realized his feelings were deeply mixed about running into the clerk on one of those brief passages: he did and he didn't want a chance meeting to occur. He wanted to communicate his desire for the clerk to come back, but without apologizing; he needed to let him know how very much he enjoyed him and their talks, but without fawning. He hated the way he considered lines to speak on a chance encounter, but at the same time he genuinely didn't know what he wanted to say. Such a meeting, if it occurred, would undoubtedly be awkward and brief.

There were, in fact, two times the librarian bumped into him, both near the office of the Clerk of the Court. One was extremely short. "How're you doin'?" was all Daniels said. The other time Rabano was sitting on one of a row of chairs in the hall outside that office. The librarian said somewhat more this time, finding words to make sure the clerk heard what he wanted him to. Rabano listened, but impassively, making no signal that could be interpreted one way or another. Having made these efforts to express himself, Daniels could only hope they'd make some difference. In terms of any resumption of the clerk visiting the library, they didn't.

Weeks went by. For two of them the librarian was far away on vacation, and the change of scene was refreshing—he rarely thought about things on the home

170

front. When he returned to work, however, he couldn't help noticing that his feelings about the clerk had shifted. Instead of being sensitive (sometimes to an excessive degree, he realized), something in him had hardened, and there were even traces of resentment. For the "friendship" to have ended suddenly because he'd uttered a single syllable didn't make sense. So now he was shifting the burden totally onto Rabano: talk about "oversensitive"! How could someone's psychology be such as to allow something so small to trigger something so large? Yes, it was all armchair speculation, Daniels knew, made in the remoteness of his own mind. Yet perhaps the clerk was in "anger management" class for good reason; perhaps in this instance he had "managed" what he was feeling pretty well. Or perhaps the cultural, social, and economic gaps between the two of them were unbridgeable, the incident having served to demonstrate that any idea to the contrary was an illusion.

As more days passed, Daniels was irritated to find the whole business still in his thoughts much more frequently than he wanted it to be. In a plainly irrational way he blamed the courthouse, because the building itself was the scene of both contact and the absence of it. When the librarian followed his routines there, he couldn't help but be within the realm of another possible encounter. After a while, not having seen him for such a long time, Daniels began to entertain the possibility that Rabano no longer worked as a clerk, that the elements he remembered in him which hated his job had at last gained the upper hand, so he'd quit, or even, for reasons the librarian was unable to imagine, been fired. Daniels reluctantly admitted to himself that the further evolution of his feelings, in conjunction with such fantasies, gave him gloating satisfaction.

Daniels knew also that in the past Rabano had sometimes come to the library in the afternoon, after Daniels' shift was over. Now he figured the clerk was coming exclusively then, in order to avoid him. One day, because it was a school holiday and in order to accommodate a request by Donovan, the head librarian, Daniels worked later than usual. It was around 12:45 when quietly—but not stealthily—through the door came Rabano.

"Henry," he said evenly, as he so often had in the past.

The librarian, seated at the front desk, looked up, registered who it was, then more or less to his own surprise said nothing.

The clerk was on his way to the middle computer and soon was seated in front of it. The librarian kept still, with his back to him. But churning inside Daniels was a maelstrom of everything that had transpired going back months. Daniels imagined that Rabano's placidity and his own upset would have been obvious to anyone stopping by to observe them. But no one else was in the library, and before long at all, the clerk having completed his business and exited without a word, Daniels was again there alone.

The next day he chose to begin his shift in a different location within the library, in the rear by the windows, near the enormous reference set called *California Forms of Pleading and Practice.* Three or four times a year a major task performed by all the staff involved removing certain outdated pages from each volume and inserting new ones the publisher sent to take their place. Edward Donovan had previously instructed his several assistants to bring

172

volumes to the front desk for this task, so that they could keep an eye on things from there. This time, in a note, he even directed that, if anyone was going to work in the rear, the assistant should leave the door positioned in such a way as to make a noise if someone entered. The generally obedient Daniels regarded the note as unnecessarily cautious. In this situation, knowing the job would soon be completed—only a few volumes were left to be updated— he chose both to do it in the back and to make no alteration of the position of the door. So he was at work, maintaining his usual concentration on the task but also looking up from time to time to determine whether anyone had entered and might need help.

"It's me, Henry," a familiar but disembodied voice said. Daniels had never seen or heard Rabano come in.

"What's happening?" Daniels replied neutrally.

"Checking my email."

This was early in the morning, remember, so the clerk's entrance destroyed the librarian's theory that he now came only in the afternoon. Daniels' reactions were again a silent tumult. In part, he felt a strange kind of excitement: he resolved to confront Rabano. But at the same time he insisted on *not* getting up immediately to go forward to the middle computer—I'm working, Daniels told himself. I'll listen for the sounds of what he's doing, I'll wait until I see him stand, ready to leave, and then I'll speak to him, from where I'm sitting. This flurry of thoughts liberated enough mental focus in him to come close to the last of the updates. Before he could reach it, though, without his noticing, the clicks of the keyboard stopped. Rabano was gone.

One morning, on his daily descent to get the mail, as Daniels was halfway down the last flight of stairs to the basement, he was stopped by the shuffling advance of the orange-clad line. The deputy tending the prisoners saw him, but Daniels stopped at the same moment, so there was no need for the deputy to issue any command. The librarian was above them, and looking down meant studying one after another moving past. A tough-looking Mexican with shaved head. A tall, skinny white guy with tattoos up and down both arms. A woman with long pretty hair but missing many teeth. A handsome kid who'd have looked more in place at a university. And there, near the end of the line, was Anthony Rabano. Daniels couldn't take his eyes off him as he came closer; the clerk's eyes looked only straight ahead. That familiar body hardly seemed restrained by the shackles binding its ankles and wrists, and with that soft step it seemed almost to glide toward the holding tank. Only as he came very close did he briefly look up.

"Henry," he said.

Acknowledgments

For their various kinds of assistance and encouragement, the author gratefully thanks the following:

Dan Barth, Tom Hine, Tom Liden
Lani Kask, Carol Rosenberg, Laura West
The Fellas (even though some are lawyers),
    especially Peter Linkow and Howard Schulman
Louise Friend and Zach Miller
Chip Freed and Rachel Michaud
Norm and Karen Rosen
Carolyn Pavlovic, Tom Anderson, Diana Ratliff
Emily Schaffner
Keith Faulder, Daniel Helsel

74747639R00122